Another Day

Bus Ride

Class Pictures

Hello. . . . Wrong Number

A Summer's Lease

A Secret Friend

A December Tale

Dorrie's Book

A Pocket Full of Seeds

The Truth About Mary Rose

The Bears' House

Marv

Peter and Veronica

Veronica Ganz

Amy and Laura

Laura's Luck

Amy Moves In

Another Day

MARILYN SACHS

Dutton Children's Books

NEW YORK

Copyright © 1997 by Marilyn Sachs

Library of Congress Cataloging-in-Publication Data

Sachs, Marilyn.
Another day / by Marilyn Sachs. — 1st ed.
p. cm.
Summary: Olivia spends her fourteenth year trying to adjust to her parents' divorce, watching the changes her widowed grandmother is going through, and discovering boys.
ISBN 0-525-45787-9
[1. Divorce—Fiction. 2. Grandmothers—Fiction.
3. Jews—United States—Fiction.] I. Title.
PZ7.S1187An 1997 [Fic]—dc21 96-45482 CIP AC

Published in the United States by Dutton Children's Books,
a division of Penguin Books USA Inc.
375 Hudson Street, New York, New York 10014

Editor: Ann Durell
Designed by Amy Berniker
Printed in U.S.A. First Edition
10 9 8 7 6 5 4 3 2 1

Gratefully, to my wise and wonderful editor,
Ann Durell—in spite of her decision to retire
. . . and to our continuing friendship

Another Day

Chapter

A COUPLE OF weeks after Olivia's mother walked out on them, her grandfather suddenly died. Then there were three of them—Olivia, her father, and her grandmother, totally overwhelmed with grief.

"I think the best thing," said her Aunt Ellen to Olivia's father, "would be for you and Olivia to go stay with Mama for a little while. She certainly needs to have somebody around, and maybe it would help the two of you forget your own problems looking after her. In a week or so, I'm sure she'll be back on her own feet again, and so will the two of you."

.   .   .

3

A year later, Olivia and her father were still living at Grandma's house, and nobody was back on his or her own feet.

"What would you like to do this weekend?" Olivia's mother asked her.

Mom had moved back to their old place, and usually, Olivia spent Saturday or Sunday of each weekend with her. Sometimes, when Nate, her mother's boyfriend, was not going to be around or was off with his own kids, she might spend the whole weekend. This was one of those times.

Olivia shrugged. "I don't care."

"Well, there's the arts and crafts fair down at Fort Mason," said her mother cheerily. "We could check it out and maybe pick up some Chanukah presents."

"Chanukah isn't for three months," Olivia said crankily. They were sitting in her room—at least it used to be her room. "Who put that dumb-looking doll on my bed?" She pointed at a small troll-doll propped up on the pillows.

"Oh, Bethy must have left it here. She slept over on Wednesday."

Olivia would have liked to pick up the doll, fling it

onto the floor, stamp on its silly face, and bury the remains deep in the garbage pail.

"Did you change the sheets?" she asked instead.

Her mother hesitated.

"I don't want to sleep on those sheets if she slept on them."

"Oh, really, Olivia," her mother said impatiently, "it was only for one night, and she never makes a fuss over changing the sheets when you've slept over for one night."

"This is supposed to be my room." Olivia's voice cracked.

"Of course it is, darling. Of course!" Her mother's voice lost its impatient edge. "It will always be your room. Of course! You know that."

She pulled Olivia over to her and kissed the top of her head. "Nate and I are thinking of going to Cabo San Lucas for a week at Christmas. How would you like to come with us, sweetheart? You'd have a marvelous time, and we'd have so much fun together."

"You said you were going to take *me* to Cabo San Lucas—just the two of us." Olivia laid her head on her mother's shoulder. It was such a familiar shoulder, its bones and indentations the same as ever and yet not the same.

"Well, yes, I did say I wanted to go with you—but Nate's never been, and neither have Bethy or Alison."

Olivia pulled up her head. "You mean they'll come, too?"

"Well, of course, darling. After all, they are his kids and he loves them a lot. But we can have so much fun. You and I can go off by ourselves sometimes, and at other times, you might enjoy getting to know the girls on your own."

"I hate them," Olivia said.

"They're lovely girls." Mom stiffened. "And they certainly aren't making the kind of fuss you're making over everything."

"No," said Olivia. "I bet they aren't. And do you know why?"

Her mother did not answer the question. She turned away her head because she knew she had walked right into the trap. For such a smart lawyer, she was forever walking into traps.

"Well, I'll tell you why. Because when their parents split, they got to stay with their mother. It wasn't their mother who left them."

"Olivia! Olivia!" her mother whispered. "I didn't leave you, darling, you know I didn't. I speak to you on the phone almost every night, and I see you nearly every weekend, and I'm always here when you need me."

"It's not the same!"

By now Olivia was crying. Even after a year, it still hurt as much as ever.

Chapter

2

OVER AND over again, Olivia tried to remember when everything had changed.

At first, she thought it had been her fault even though both Mom and Dad insisted it had not. And yet, she kept remembering back to the time when she was nearly thirteen, and suddenly one day, her temperature shot up to 104 degrees just before bedtime.

Dad was sitting on her bed, and she was nestling under Dad's arm, snuggling into his side. He had just spoken to her pediatrician, Dr. Green. "He thinks it's a virus. He said to keep giving her Tylenol, and make sure she drinks fluids—the usual. But, if it's still up tomorrow, to bring her in."

"Poor baby!" Mom rested a cool hand on her hot head.

"Would you be able to take tomorrow off, Maggie?" Dad asked. "I'm meeting Bob Simmons about an idea I have for some new computer software, and my mother is tied up."

"I can't imagine where Olivia picked it up," Mom began stroking her arm. "Unless it was at your mother's house on Shabbat. Zack had a cold, if you remember, and your sister kept saying it was nothing. She always says it's nothing when it's her kids. Anyway, Adam, I have the Forbes case tomorrow in court, so I can't stay home. You'll have to put off your meeting with Bob for another day."

Mom was a lawyer. Dad mostly worked at home. He was an artist, but recently he'd begun developing computer software.

"I'm thirsty," Olivia said.

"I'll get you some water, honey." Dad jumped up, and Olivia slipped back heavily onto her pillow.

She must have dozed off, but suddenly she knew that Dad had not brought her any water. Her throat began feeling as if she had swallowed pins, and she was about to call out. Then she heard them arguing in the kitchen.

"Oh, stop making a fuss!" Mom was saying. "What's the big deal, anyway?"

"Because," Dad answered. "I've already told you. He's leaving town after tomorrow for a few weeks, and it's the only day he could see me. It could mean something big for me if he likes my idea."

"You always say that," said Mom. "It's always going to be something big, but it never is."

"I'm always the one," Dad said, "who's expected to take off—to stop whatever I'm doing when she's sick. It's always me, or my mother. I'm just asking you to do it this one time."

"Well, Adam, I don't have to remind you, do I, that I'm the one who's making the money in this family. I'm the one who has the steady paycheck."

"Which you do remind me—over and over again."

But then they both saw her standing there in the doorway. She must have looked astonished, she supposed, because they hardly ever argued. At least, she hardly ever heard them argue.

They turned. She remembered how they both turned. Dad was holding a glass of water in his hand, and she remembered how some of it splashed on the floor, and how all three of them began laughing.

She remembered, too, that Dad must have cancelled his meeting the next day, because he was the one who stayed home with her, as he usually did.

Olivia knew her family was different from most families, where fathers worked as well as mothers or worked instead of mothers. Dad was always the one who came up to school to speak to her teachers or to watch her play volleyball when she was on the team. Dad was the one she cried all over when somebody made fun of her, and Dad was the one she called out for in the middle of the night after a nightmare.

Dad had always been there when she needed him. But then, so had Mom. At least, Olivia had always thought so before Mom walked out on them. When Mom came into a room, everything speeded up and brightened. She spoke quickly, moved quickly, and made decisions that sparked their lives. Olivia was so proud of Mom—of her pretty face, the way she smoothed her hair, the way she laughed, and the way their weekends were spent in a whirlwind of exciting projects.

Before Mom left, they had been restoring their new

home—stripping wallpaper off walls, painting rooms, refinishing woodwork, and laying out a garden. Her mother had persuaded her father to buy a small house not far from her grandparents' larger house. It was a fixer-upper, and most weekends they spent fixing it up.

And they had. The little, ratty house now had become so beautiful that there were times Olivia could hardly believe it when she opened the door to *her* house, and stood looking into *her* pretty living room with its inviting window seat in the bay window. And then *her* own small but wonderful room with its yellow walls, white trim, and tiny balcony overlooking the garden!

Olivia remembered the time her father had dug up a locked box in the garden when he was pulling up some ugly shrubs. She remembered how he yelled for the two of them, who were washing the funny old chandelier in the hall, to come outside immediately.

"It's a treasure," Olivia cried, feeling the cold fog wrapping around her and shivering deliciously.

"Open it! Open it, Adam!" her mother shouted, also excited, her cheeks very pink. Mom's cheeks always turned pink whenever she was particularly happy or excited.

Dad had to break the lock, and as he opened the box, they nearly fell over each other looking inside. But all they found was an old, scruffy teddy bear wrapped in a doll's pink blanket.

Mom thought it must have come from a time when people got rid of toys their children had kept during bouts of polio or some other contagious disease. Dad thought maybe it was like Puff the Magic Dragon—a child had outgrown a once loved toy and ceremoniously buried it. Olivia remembered wondering—and sometimes she still wondered—if it was a clue, maybe to a treasure, and that they needed to look for other buried boxes that would contain other clues.

And then—just as their house was finished, and was so beautiful that the three of them had barely stopped marvelling and congratulating each other—Mom began slipping away.

Neither of them—Olivia nor Dad—had noticed at first, but, Olivia remembered now how Mom began working longer and longer hours. And she travelled more. Of course, she had always travelled, but suddenly, it was often, and mostly on weekends.

And then—all of a sudden, she was gone.

Grandma said terrible things. This was before Grandpa died. She called Mom names that Olivia would not have believed Grandma even knew the meaning of. She told Olivia and her father that they both were better off without a woman like that, a woman whose husband was only too good, who waited on her hand and foot, who never said a mean word to her. And a daughter—one daughter, one child, Olivia—a child whom any parent would die for! Grandma said she never wanted Mom to speak to her again. Never!

As the time passed, Olivia came to believe it was not her fault, and yet she kept remembering that night she ran the high fever. The memory was beginning to slip away, too, and sometimes she wasn't sure if it was Dad who was holding the glass of water or if it was Mom.

At first, when Mom left, Olivia was too upset to feel anything other than sorrow and confusion. The months passed, but it still didn't get any better, only now Olivia felt increasingly angry and frightened.

Dad bought a new computer and spent more and more time in his room. They hardly ever talked about Mom anymore, but Olivia knew Dad thought about her all the time. And so did she.

Chapter

3

GRANDMA WAS the one who had changed the most. And living there in the same house with her, Olivia had watched it happen, helplessly.

Before Grandpa died, Grandma had been a ball of fire. That's what Aunt Ellen always called her—not always admiringly, either. Grandma had been into everything—especially everything involving her children and grandchildren. Last year, a few months before Grandpa died, Grandma had made all the arrangements for Olivia's bat mitzvah party.

Mom had suggested a small catered affair at the temple, as most of Olivia's friends were having, but Grandma said no. She said more than no.

"My oldest grandchild!" Grandma said. "Absolutely not! It will be held here, downstairs in the family room and garden if the weather is good. And no catering— except maybe the knishes. I'll do all the cooking myself."

"I suppose you'll need help," Aunt Ellen said carefully.

"Of course I'll need help," Grandma told her. "Maggie will help, naturally, and so will you, and we'll hire a few high school kids from Enterprise."

"That's okay with me," Aunt Ellen continued, still carefully, "as long as next year, when Judy is bat mitzvahed, you'll do the same for her."

"Bite your tongue!" Grandma said. "Of course I will. You should know better than even to bring it up. I love all my darling, wonderful grandchildren the same. When? Tell me when, did I ever even once show any favoritism?"

Aunt Ellen did not answer. She knew as well as Olivia—as well as everybody in the family—that Olivia had always been Grandma's favorite.

"When Judy is bat mitzvahed next year, we'll hold exactly the same kind of party here, and then when Zack and Seth are bar mitzvahed, it will be exactly the same too, God willing."

. . .

But God was not willing, and Judy's bat mitzvah party was held in the temple with catered food.

"I'm not complaining," Aunt Ellen said. "If Papa was alive, I'm sure she would have made the party. But that's always the way it turns out when it comes to me and my children."

"I'm sorry," Olivia's father said. "It would have been much better for Mama if she could have made the party."

"Actually," Olivia said, "Judy's party was a lot bigger than mine. And you had music, and everybody danced. And Grandma paid for it—didn't she?"

"That's not the point at all, Olivia," her aunt said.

"Judy told me she liked her party better than mine," Olivia continued. "She said she could invite all of her friends, and she enjoyed the fancy food more, and the champagne. Grandma didn't have any champagne at my party."

"Judy's got a big mouth," said Aunt Ellen, "and so do you, Olivia. But anyway, Adam, what are we going to do about Mama?"

"Do?"

"Adam," Aunt Ellen said impatiently, "I know you're still not all over—Well, you know what I mean," nodding significantly at Olivia.

"No," Olivia said. "He's not over Mom and neither am I."

"Olivia," said her aunt, "I wish you wouldn't keep interrupting. I was talking to your father, you know."

Dad sighed and pulled Olivia over towards him. "Don't pick on her, Ellen," he said. "She's been having a rough time, too."

"I'm not criticizing Olivia," Aunt Ellen said. "Listen, she's my niece, and I love her very much. I know it hasn't been easy for her, but we will have to do something about Mama."

That's when Grandma came into the room, all dressed up and smiling vaguely.

"Mama," Aunt Ellen asked. "Are you ready?"

Grandma sat down next to Olivia, and looked toward the door.

"Mama, today's the luncheon the Sisterhood is giving for the new members of the congregation. We're already a little late."

"Oh, yes," Grandma said, still sitting.

"I spoke to Joan Miller, and she's hoping you'll be able to help out for next month's book sale."

"No," Grandma said, still watching the door. "I don't think so."

"Mama, you have to try. It's not like you. It's not

good, Mama. You used to be the president of the Sister-hood. You used to bake all the cakes for their parties and luncheons. You used to be in charge of the volunteers."

Grandma nodded. "I can't," she said softly, still smiling.

"Listen, Mama." Aunt Ellen moved her chair closer to her mother. "You can't bring back the past. Yesterday is yesterday, and today is today. You can't just sit around, and do nothing. You have to forget about the past and move on. You have to try." She looked up at Olivia and her father. "Everybody has to try. If you don't want to work in the Sisterhood anymore—I know, Mama. Papa was so active in the temple. Maybe you need to find a new interest. Maybe you'd enjoy taking a course at the Fromm Institute. They give wonderful courses for seniors. Look, I brought you a catalog, and you'd meet some new people your own age."

"I don't think so, dear," Grandma said, still looking at the door. "But it's nice of you to think of me. You're a good girl."

Most days, Grandma just dressed up in one of her pret-tiest outfits and sat in a chair watching the door. Olivia knew her grandmother was watching for Grandpa. Some-times, Olivia sat with her, also watching the door even though she knew, of course, that Grandpa would never come back through it.

At first she tried to get Grandma to talk. That had never been a problem in the past. If anything, Grandma talked too much—mostly about everyday matters, or temple affairs, or her plans for, and opinions of, various members of the family. Sometimes Grandma also talked about how she and Grandpa met. Both of them had been born in Germany and hadn't come over to the United States until after World War II. They had been in hiding all that time when they were children and were always hungry. Grandma used to tell how their families had run away to Belgium, but then the Nazis conquered Belgium and rounded up the Jews to take them to concentration camps. The Nazis hunted for them while they hid out in different houses, and one by one, different members of their families were taken. One terrible story she told was how Grandpa hung from his fingertips from a window outside of a house the Nazis were searching while she hid under a heap of coal in the cellar.

It was a terrifying story, but Olivia was not terrified —because she knew Grandma and Grandpa would escape, fall in love, come safely to America, and become her own happy, comfortable grandparents. But nowadays, Grandma just sat silently watching the door, and Olivia's fears began growing because she did not know how everything would end.

Once, when she was about three, a big dog had run after her, and bit her on the thigh. It was her most frightening memory—running away from the dog, hearing its snarls, feeling its wild breath on her legs and, then, its sharp teeth. Now, as she sat helplessly beside her silent grandmother, she felt the same kind of terror.

Olivia worried about her father, too. Suddenly, he was like somebody she hardly knew. He had a room full of computers now and spent most of his time inside it. Like the princess who had to spin a room full of straw into gold, lately Dad had been trying to spin his straw into gold and had even sold a couple of art programs to an educational computer software company.

"Well, it's about time," said Olivia's mother, on another weekend. "He never took himself seriously before. Maybe it's a good thing—for his career, I mean. He might even make some money for a change."

"It's not a good thing," Olivia told her. "We always had enough money, and we were happy. Dad and I were happy. We thought you were, too."

"Well, I was, darling, I was . . . for a while. But, you know, you're only fourteen, and—"

"I hate when people tell me I'm only fourteen or I'm too young to understand. It's not fair."

"Okay! Okay! Let me try again. Your father and I were very young when we married. We met in college, and I guess I was his first girlfriend. And I was really impressed with him. He was—I guess he still is—a talented artist. But, of course, you can't just live on talent when you have a family. We were both only twenty-one when we married. Olivia—make sure, Olivia, you don't jump into marriage with the first guy you meet. Take your time. Wait until you're—thirty at least."

"So I'll end up with someone like Nate? No thanks! Dad is the nicest man I know," Olivia said loyally. "Nobody else has a father like mine."

"He is a nice man," her mother agreed, "and I'll always love him. But he's also, well, always lacked drive. I didn't realize when I was younger that I wanted more out of life. I didn't always want to stay in the same place. I wanted to grow. . . . Nate's like that, too. He's ambitious. He'll make partner one of these days. Maybe I will, too, especially now that I have somebody who's encouraging me."

"So you can both make a lot of money," Olivia suggested bitterly. "Well, I guess you're going to be very busy—you and Nate. And I guess you're not going to have much time for me."

"No, no, darling, you don't understand."

"No, I don't," Olivia said fiercely. "I don't understand why you just walked out. Why you . . . why you . . . never even thought about taking me with you."

"Olivia, darling, don't you see—your dad was the one who always took care of you. And your grandmother, too. I'm away so much. And I always wanted the best for you. But, darling, you know I'm always there for you when you need me. And we always have so much fun together. That's not going to change."

Mom tried to pull Olivia toward her, but Olivia shook her off. "You just don't want me to interfere with Nate and his nerdy daughters. They're the ones you care about now."

"Why don't we decide what we want to do today," Mom said brightly. "Would you like to go shopping? I think they're having a big sale at Esprit."

Chapter

LAURA FRANKLIN, Olivia's best friend, had a different kind of family from Olivia's. Her mother gave some piano lessons, but mostly stayed home with Laura and her younger brother, Todd. Her father was a flutist with the symphony. He didn't baby-sit very much, except when he supervised his children's practicing.

Laura and Olivia had been friends for a long time and agreed about most things. There was one thing, however, they did not agree on at all—Laura's dog, Henry.

"Did you put him outside?" Olivia wanted to know as she peered nervously around her friend before coming through the door of Laura's house.

"No, but Todd took him out to the dog run at the park."
Olivia hesitated. "When will he be back?"

"Oh, will you stop it," Laura snapped, yanking her friend into the house. "Henry is the gentlest dog in the world. He's even afraid of cats."

"But he barks and jumps on me," Olivia said.

"He barks and jumps on everybody," Laura explained. "That only means he likes you and he's friendly. You've got to get over your nutty fear of dogs."

"Well, it's because—"

"I know. I know. A big dog chased you and bit your backside when you were three, and you never forgot it. But that happened a long time ago. You have to forget about the past and just go on."

"That's what my Aunt Ellen keeps telling my grandmother," Olivia said.

"How is your grandmother?"

"The same. Today she dressed up in the outfit she bought for Passover the last year Grandpa was alive. It's a blue silk dress with a matching jacket. Then she sat around watching the door, as usual. It's terrible, and I just wish I knew what to do."

"Can't your father take her places?"

"Sometimes he does, but most of the time he's sitting in his room playing with his computers."

"He should go out on dates," Laura said. "My Uncle Fred—his wife walked out, too—and he was like a zombie for most of that year. But then he met this real nice woman on BART—she didn't know how to get to Walnut Creek, and he told her how. And then her train was late, and they talked for twenty minutes on the platform, and he ended up going to Walnut Creek with her."

"My father never rides BART. He hardly ever goes out of the house except to go shopping. Besides, he's not interested in dates. He keeps saying Mom will come back. He's waiting for Mom."

Laura didn't say anything. She took her violin bow out of its case and began fiddling with it.

"Look!" Olivia insisted, "There's a good chance she will come back. She keeps saying she loves Dad, and that she always will. Now that he sold some computer programs and even made a little money, I think she's really impressed. And besides, her boyfriend, Nate is a jerk. I hate him and his dumb kids."

Laura just kept loosening her bow and remained silent.

"You don't know everything," Olivia snapped. "So stop giving me advice."

"I didn't say anything." Laura put the bow back into

its case. "Anyway, I want you to see what my grandmother sent me for Rosh Hashanah."

Laura had a white, Jewish grandmother just like Olivia, but the rest of Laura's family were African American and Methodist. But every year at Rosh Hashanah, her Jewish grandmother, who lived in Cincinnati, sent all her grandchildren presents.

"My grandmother gives us presents at Chanukah," Olivia said.

"Well, mine does too, but she also gives us presents at Rosh Hashanah."

"What did she send you?"

"Take a look at me," Laura said. "Don't you notice anything different?"

Olivia looked at her friend's pretty face, at her long eye lashes, and down at her denim shirt and black jeans.

"I don't see anything different."

"You're not looking." Laura leaned forward, and tossed her head from side to side. Something sparkled in her ears.

"They're not real diamonds, are they?" Olivia asked.

"Of course not, silly. They're some kind of crystals. When I move my head fast, they look like little rainbows. Watch!"

"They're nice," Olivia said without much enthusiasm. She never wore earrings herself, because she didn't have the courage to have her ears pierced. It was one of the few things she didn't like to admit to Laura.

The outside door opened, and Henry came bounding noisily into the room.

"Oh, no! Oh, no!" Olivia screamed, leaping up and trying to hide behind Laura.

"Down, Henry, down!" Laura ordered.

Todd, Laura's brother, was laughing. "Boy, you are some chicken, Olivia," he said. "Nobody's afraid of Henry. You should have seen the way this little puppy at the dog run scared him silly."

Henry's tail was thumping the floor, and he was making a pleading sound in his throat.

"Please get him out of here, Todd! Please!" Olivia begged, her arms tightly wound around Laura.

"She's hopeless," Laura grumbled. "Put him in the kitchen, Todd, and stop squashing me, Olivia."

"Anyway, I need to talk to you about something else," Laura continued, after Henry and Todd had departed, and Olivia had disentangled herself. "There's going to be a Christmas recital for advanced students, and my father is expecting me to play. I told him I don't want to, but he says I have to."

Laura played the violin. Her music teacher held different recitals during the year, and as long as Olivia had known her, Laura always tried to get out of performing.

"I can't figure out why you never want to play," Olivia said. "Everybody says you're great—that you're exceptionally talented."

"I know," Laura admitted. "I am. But I'm nervous when I have to play before people. I like to play by myself or even with my Dad, but I always feel like throwing up when I have to play in front of an audience. And it's getting worse."

"You'll never be able to be a violinist if you don't play in front of people," Olivia said. "You can't be a professional musician if you only play for yourself. And I know you want to be a violinist. Don't you?"

"Last year," Laura said, "I really messed up. My fingers got so stiff, and I left out a whole passage in the middle. It was terrible."

"You'll get over it," Olivia said. "The more you play in front of people, the easier it will get."

"You know something, Olivia." Laura hesitated.

"What?"

"Well . . . I think I want to give it up. I think . . . I don't want to play the violin anymore."

"You're kidding! You've been playing the violin ever

since you were, what, six or seven? I remember you walking around with a tiny, little violin even before we became friends."

"I know! I know!" Laura shook her head. "Olivia, I really want to give it up, but I don't know what to tell my dad. He's so set on me being a musician, just like him. He's been disappointed because Todd never took his music seriously, and I know he likes to think I'll carry on the family tradition. But I don't want to, and what should I do?"

"I don't know," Olivia said, beginning to feel a deep sorrow.

"Well, I mean, parents always expect so much from their kids. My mother expects me to be on the honor roll each term, and my Dad wants me to be some kind of serious violin prodigy. How can you tell them—hey, get off my back. I know you love me, but it's my life. Let me go!"

"I don't know," Olivia repeated. She jumped up. "I have to go home," she said. She was close to tears.

"What's the big hurry?" Laura said. "I thought we were going to hang out this afternoon."

"No! I have to go. Right away." Olivia grabbed her jacket, and ran out the door as quickly as she could. Later, maybe, she would call Laura and try to explain.

She hurried through the streets, but the expectations of Laura's parents, like a monster dog, hurried after her, panting and snapping at her heels.

When was the last time her own parents had held any high expectations about her? Even though she wasn't a musical prodigy, she was usually on the honor roll, and there had been a time when her parents' expectations about her achieving great and remarkable goals had always assured her that she would. And, like Laura, she *had* worried from time to time about disappointing them.

Olivia was almost running now. For over a year, neither parent seemed to have any kind of expectations about her. And on her side, she did not have to worry about disappointing them because, she suddenly realized, how much each of them had disappointed her.

Chapter 5

FRIDAY NIGHT, the beginning of Shabbat, had always been so much a part of Olivia's life that she never even thought about it before Grandpa died, and Mom walked out on them.

Then, Grandma lit the candles just before dusk, covered her head, and rocked back and forth as she prayed. Even as a small child, Olivia knew that Grandma was talking to God, and it comforted her to know that God had to be listening.

Friday night, the whole family had always gathered for the traditional Shabbat dinner—Grandpa, Grandma,

Aunt Ellen, Uncle Daniel, Judy, Zack, Seth, Mom, Dad, and herself. Sometimes other relatives showed up, but except for sickness or vacations, the core of ten was always present—all dressed up and shiny faced.

Usually Grandma baked the challah herself and made a special dinner. Sometimes it might be the traditional soup, matzo balls, chicken, potato kugel, honeyed carrots, salad, and sponge cake. Other times she might make brisket or stuffed breast of veal. Grandma's voice rang out through the house, encircling the children as they played, and summoning them all, finally, to the big table in the dining room.

Grandpa "presided" and Grandma "provided." That's what Dad always said. Everybody was expected to eat.

"What's wrong, Olivia?" Grandma might say. "Is the chicken tough?"

"No, Grandma, but I already ate a drumstick."

"Here, eat another one, and, Zack, you're not eating any salad. You have to eat some vegetables if you want to grow up big and strong."

After the meal, everybody had a package of food to take home—enough for at least another meal for the next night.

Now, they still gathered to celebrate Shabbat, but their number had dwindled to eight.

"Mama," Aunt Ellen said, "aren't you going to light the candles? It's nearly dark."

"Oh, yes. Of course." Grandma covered her head, lit the candles, and stood silently in front of them—not rocking, not praying, not talking to God.

"He hears what's in her heart," Aunt Ellen whispered. Then she said out loud, in a fake, cheery voice, "Okay, kids, let's get the table set. I'm sure everybody's starving."

Now it was either Uncle Dan or Dad who presided at the head of the table and said the kiddush over the wine with the store-bought challah.

Grandma didn't provide anymore. For a while, Aunt Ellen cooked the Shabbat meal, but lately, Mrs. Frobish, the cleaning lady, who used to come only on Wednesdays to clean, now came on Friday afternoons as well, to do the cooking. Mrs. Frobish wasn't a very good cook and didn't bother preparing any of Grandma's special dishes. Usually Mrs. Frobish cooked chicken, rice, and plain, steamed carrots. Aunt Ellen generally bought a cake from the bakery.

"So, Olivia," said Uncle Dan, as all of them were

chewing away at Mrs. Frobish's food, "what's happening with you? You're unusually quiet tonight."

"Nothing," Olivia said. She pecked away at her food.

"Getting lots of A's in everything as usual?"

"I don't always get A's in everything, and, this term, I'm probably failing algebra."

Her father looked up. "Failing algebra?" he repeated.

"And I'm not playing volleyball anymore, because the coach keeps me on the bench."

"Not playing volleyball?" her father repeated again.

"And it doesn't make any difference at all to my parents."

Olivia picked up a radish and tore a huge piece out of it, although she loathed radishes. It tasted disgusting, but she knew she could not spit it out without losing her dignity.

Nobody said anything for as long as she chewed. Everybody else, except for her grandmother, was looking at her father who was looking at her.

"And another thing," she announced to the quiet table, "My friend, Laura Franklin, is planning to give up her violin."

"Who?" Seth asked.

"My friend, Laura Franklin, who is a very talented

musician. It will probably break her father's heart if she gives it up. Her father really cares very, very deeply about her playing. And her mother really cares about her getting on the honor roll. Some parents are deeply involved in their kids' lives."

"Not on the volleyball team?" Dad shook his head. "You always had the best serve."

"Not anymore," Olivia told him. "That little snake Deborah Fine must have grown a foot over the summer, and Selina Matthews—she's new—slams it so hard, nobody can get it back."

"In any case," Aunt Ellen said, "I don't think you can ever accuse your father of not being interested or involved in you. I always used to point out to Uncle Dan how your father always showed up for all your games."

"Not anymore."

"And always took such an interest in everything you did. And, of course, your mother, too, when she was home. Naturally, she's a lawyer and lawyers work twelve-hour days, so . . ."

"So do physicians," Uncle Dan reminded her. "Sometimes you forget that I work a twelve-hour day, too, often more."

"Well, nobody is interested in me anymore," Olivia muttered as her aunt turned angrily toward her husband.

"Dad's busy playing with his computers all the time now, and Mom . . ." She could feel the tears gathering up behind her eyes, and she jumped up and hurried out of the room as Aunt Ellen said to Uncle Dan, "Well, let me remind you that I work a lot more than a twelve-hour day!"

Chapter

6

UNCLE DAN had sent Grandma for a bunch of medical tests, and the reports had all come back. Physically, Grandma was in great shape for a woman of her age—heart, lungs, nose, ears, eyes—even her weight—all working as they should.

"Dr. Miller says you're in wonderful shape," Aunt Ellen told Grandma. "He says you could pass for a woman twenty years younger."

Today, Grandma wore her lavender-striped matching skirt and blouse. Her face was carefully made up and her large pearl earrings matched the pearl pin at her throat.

Grandma stiffened because she heard a key in the

lock, but it only turned out to be Dad coming back from shopping.

"Hi, Adam," Aunt Ellen said as Dad came into the living room, carrying two large bags from Safeway.

"Hi, Ellen. What's doing?"

"Nothing special. I was just telling Mama the reports came back from Dr. Miller, and they were all excellent. Actually, her blood pressure is even better than before. But . . ."

"That's great," Dad said, putting down his packages. "But what?"

"Mama, he said he talked to you."

"Oh, yes," Grandma said. "A very nice man. He talks a little fast, but I understood."

"He said he told you he advised an antidepressant."

Grandma shrugged. "What's it like outside, Adam?"

"Kind of windy, but not bad. Would you like to go out?"

"No. No. I just wondered." Grandma's eyes moved back to the door.

"Mama—Dan agrees—and I know he's told you this lots of times. You should take an antidepressant. Papa's been dead for over a year now, and you just have to make a little more of an effort."

"There's nothing wrong with me," Grandma said.

"There's nothing *physically* wrong with you," Aunt Ellen qualified, "but you're not yourself, Mama. You just sit around and do nothing. When did you ever sit around? When?"

"Papa always wanted me to take it easier," Grandma said. "I told him when you retire I'll take it easy. So . . ."

"How about going for a walk?" Dad suggested. "We could go down to Spreckels Lake. It's so sheltered there, you hardly feel the wind."

Aunt Ellen looked at her watch. "I can't go, Adam. I just stopped by on my way home from the beauty parlor, and I need to do some shopping. But, Mama, why don't you go? You haven't been out of the house for days."

Surprisingly, Grandma said, "Okay. I'll get my coat. I'll be right back."

"That was a good suggestion, Adam," Aunt Ellen whispered when her mother left the room. "She has to get out." She smiled at Dad. "Do you remember how she was always at us to go out and get some fresh air? And you always wanted to stay home, and draw pictures."

"I remember." Dad and Aunt Ellen smiled and nodded at each other.

Brother and sister, Olivia thought bitterly. They have each other. They don't have to depend on parents. I'm all by myself.

Dad was looking at her. "You come too, Olivia. I want to talk to you."

Grandma returned, wearing her beige three-quarter coat and a purple-and-pink scarf.

"You look nice, Mama." Aunt Ellen kissed her. "You need to get out more. Spreckels Lake is a good place for you. It's close by and it's safe. You can just walk right in at Thirty-sixth Avenue, and there's always lots of people there."

"I know," Grandma said. "Papa and I used to walk around Spreckels Lake all the time."

"I didn't know that," Aunt Ellen said.

"We'd go out, sometimes after he came home from work or maybe early on a Sunday morning."

"He said he needed the exercise," Grandma told Olivia and Dad as they walked around the lake. "He told me it was half a mile around, and he liked to walk at least two times around. But sometimes he got tired." Grandma sniffed the air. "It's nice here," she said. "And it smells so good."

"You can come yourself, Mama," Dad said. "Like Ellen told you, there's always plenty of people here." He motioned to the groups of men and women, mostly older, sitting on the benches, sailing model boats, walking dogs, wheeling baby carriages, playing dominoes. "You don't have to wait to go out with me or . . . with anybody else."

"I think I'll sit down now, Adam," Grandma said, moving towards an empty bench, "but you and Olivia go and walk some more."

Dad hesitated.

"Go, Adam. I'm just a little tired. Go!"

"Well, maybe just one more time around. Come on Olivia." They looked back over their shoulders as they walked off and waved at Grandma, sitting on the bench, but she was looking off in another direction.

"Actually," Dad said, "I really wanted a chance to talk to you, Olivia." He slowed down and put his arm around Olivia's shoulder. "I didn't like what you said last night. I didn't like your implication that I don't care about you and that your mother doesn't either."

"Well, it's true," Olivia said in a sour voice. She looked back again at Grandma sitting alone on the bench, watching something on the empty path. "She keeps watching for Grandpa," Olivia said. "She knows he's not coming, but she's waiting for him anyway."

"I called your mother this morning." Dad sounded almost shy. "I told her what you said last night, and she was really upset. I know you'll be spending the day with her tomorrow, but she . . . she suggested maybe the three of us should get together and try to work this out."

"Dad!"

Dad's face was struggling to keep itself calm, but his mouth began turning upwards. "And then I said maybe we could all go to Rossi's for brunch, like we used to, and sit out in the garden. Remember, Olivia, it used to be our favorite place."

"It's still my favorite place, even though we haven't been back since Mom left." Olivia wanted to jump up and down. She had a deep, deep, happy feeling that suddenly everything was going to be all right again. "But did she say yes, Dad?"

"Uh-huh." Dad's smile covered his whole face. " 'What a wonderful idea!' That's what she said. 'Olivia will love it,' she said. 'And they never rush you there, so we can really talk our heads off. Olivia will like that, too.' "

"Dad, you should wear that wild Jackson Pollock shirt Mom bought you a few years ago. She always loved that shirt, and you hardly ever wore it."

"I don't know where it is," Dad said. "I can't remember if I packed it when we moved in with Grandma."

"We'll look for it when we get home. Oh, Dad, I'm so happy! Maybe she's ready to come back. Maybe she's sick of Nate and his dumb kids. Maybe—"

"Now, Olivia, I don't want you to get your hopes up. She did sound like she was happy to go with us to Rossi's, but, Olivia, I really don't want you to think everything's going to work out."

Dad's beaming face looked to Olivia as if he thought everything was going to work out, too. She pressed his hand, and then she looked across the sparkling waters of the lake to where Grandma was sitting and she waved again. But Grandma didn't see her. Grandma was still looking off in another direction.

Olivia sniffed the air. "Mm!" she said. "It does smell good here, doesn't it, Dad?"

Chapter

7

MOM WAS sitting there, waiting for them, when they arrived at Rossi's. Olivia noticed that Mom was wearing a red shirt and a red scarf. She hoped it was because Mom knew that red was Dad's favorite color.

"Hello, darling," she said, reaching out to Olivia and pulling her close. She kissed Olivia's cheek and held her tight. Olivia laid her head on Mom's shoulder and wished hard inside herself, Come home, Mom! Please! Come home!

"Adam."

"Hi, Maggie."

Her parents were nodding at each other, but neither of them made a move. Olivia raised her head from Mom's shoulder. Kiss! Kiss! Kiss! she wished, and Mom did move forward and kiss Dad's cheek.

Then the three of them moved around noisily, seating themselves and talking about was the table okay and who wanted to sit in the sun and should they take the other table over in the corner.

"No!" Olivia said. "Let's stay here. This is the table we always wanted to sit at. This is our table."

Her parents quieted down, and neither of them said anything. So Olivia began. "I love it here," she said fervently. "It's my favorite restaurant. I even like the food."

Mom laughed. It felt like old times—good, old times.

"How's your mother, Adam?" she asked.

"The same."

"I miss her," Mom said. "I really do. I miss the Shabbat meals. I miss all the hustle and bustle and the good food and all the racket."

"It's not the same," Olivia said. "I told you Grandma doesn't cook anymore, and the food is terrible. But, Mom, you could come and cook. I could help you. Please, Mom, why don't you just come Friday. Please!"

"Oh, darling," Mom said. "I can't, darling."

"You mean because you can't get off from work," Dad

said quickly. "Well, it's all right, Maggie. Now that Ellen's gone back to teaching full-time, she can't usually spare the time either. That's why Mrs. Frobish is doing the cooking. But it's not really that bad."

"Just this once, Mom! Just take the time off this once, and I'll never ask you again."

"Oh, darling, I can't. I really can't."

Then the waiter came, and they all ordered, but not the way they used to. In the old days Mom and Olivia always ordered waffles, and Dad always ordered an omelet with Italian sausages. Today, Olivia ordered the waffles, but Mom had a poached egg on whole wheat toast, and Dad had a scone and fruit salad. In spite of that, Olivia remained hopeful and ate most of her waffles while her parents talked about their work and their friends and should Dad ask the waiter for more coffee.

Mom finally came to the point. "Olivia," she said, "I've been crying off and on since Dad called yesterday."

Olivia stopped eating and waited, her fork hanging in the air.

"I think it's time we really dealt with our feelings honestly and decided what would be best for all of us."

"I know what would be best for me," said Olivia. "It would be best for me if we could be a real family again. And Dad. For Dad, too. I know how he feels."

Dad didn't say anything. He didn't have to. The way he looked at Mom—she had to understand.

Mom put out her hand and took Olivia's. Mom's hand was trembling. "I can't," she whispered. "I can't."

Then Dad held up his hand and signaled the waiter. "More coffee, please," he called.

Olivia pulled away her hand. "Why not?" she asked. "You said you've been crying, and Dad and I are miserable. Why not?"

Tears began rolling down Mom's face. "I can't darling, but let me tell you that I know it's all going to work out. It's all going to be different. Let me just . . ." Mom pulled some tissues out of her purse, and sunk her face into them as the waiter awkwardly poured coffee.

Olivia set her fork down and watched her mother cry. Mom's shoulders were heaving now, and Dad murmured something like "Maggie! It's okay, Maggie!"

But it wasn't okay. Olivia felt a cruel, deep fury rising up inside her as she looked at the sobbing woman who, she knew, was about to say something that would make everything worse.

"I'm sorry." Her mother finally lifted her soggy face out of the tissues. "But . . ." She smiled a shaky smile. "I think all three of us needed this to clarify the situation.

I think maybe we've all been frozen in some kind of time warp, and it's important to make a real move."

Olivia said nothing. She heard her father's coffee cup clink in its saucer, but she kept her eyes on her mother's face and waited.

"I think, Olivia, that you need to face up to the fact that your father and I will never get together again. Never! But—and you should certainly know that each of us loves you and will always be there for you, that nothing has changed in that respect. But . . ."

"Are you finished?" Olivia asked in a frozen voice.

"No—not yet," said her mother. "Nate and I have decided to get married as soon as the divorce is final. Adam, I'm planning to move out of our house right away. By next weekend, if I can. I think now it was a mistake for me to move back there, because it wasn't good for Olivia, seeing me in her old home. It didn't help her accept that the past was over. We've decided to move to Mill Valley. We've actually put a down payment on a little house in a big, beautiful garden. I always wanted a real garden, and Olivia, there's a great deck to loaf on, and you and I can swim over at—"

Olivia stood up. "I hate you!" she said. "I don't want to see you ever again."

"Olivia!" Dad stood up, too, and tried to pull her down into her chair. "Come on, honey, just try—"

"No, I won't!" Olivia shouted. "She never thinks of anybody but herself."

Mom stood up, too, and reached both arms out. "Please, Olivia, just let me explain." Her fingers were curling around Olivia's arm, but Olivia shook them off, pushed back her chair, and ran out of Rossi's.

She wasn't crying. She was too angry to cry.

"Olivia! Olivia!" She heard Dad, running behind her, and she stopped and waited for him.

"Olivia!" He caught up and wrapped his arms around her.

"I don't want to see her or talk to her ever again," she said, burying her face in his stupid Jackson Pollock shirt. "And I think you should take off this dumb shirt and throw it in Spreckels Lake."

"Okay!" Dad agreed, and started laughing. She looked up and laughed too, even though the cruel, deep fury was still there and stayed on and on and on.

Chapter

LAURA WAS supposed to tell her father that she planned on giving up the violin. She planned on telling him Tuesday evening just before dinner.

Olivia called her at twenty minutes to nine.

"Well?" she asked. "What did he say?"

"Just a minute," Laura said. "Let me close the door first."

Olivia settled back on her bed and waited. She arranged a pillow more comfortably because she knew Laura would go into all the details of what she said and what he said. Olivia felt happy in advance for Laura. She felt happy for herself, too, because once Laura gave up practicing, they would have more time together.

"Hello!" Laura again.

"So?"

"Well—I didn't tell him yet."

"How come?"

"It just didn't work out. He has an ear infection, and he's worried about being able to play this week. His ear hurts him, and the doctor thinks—"

"So when are you going to tell him?"

"I guess I'll have to wait until he's feeling better. Anyway, you'll be the first person to know when it's over."

"Don't forget. Anyway, let's get together tomorrow after school. I know I finish earlier than you Wednesdays, but I'll wait for you in the library."

"No, I can't. I have to practice that new sonata my music teacher gave me for the recital. I have my lesson on Thursday, and I need to work it over a little more."

"But if you're going to give it up, why do you need to practice?"

Laura didn't answer.

"Laura?"

"Oh, right, Olivia. I don't know why. It's stupid, but I do. Anyway, did your mother call again?"

"Sure. Every day. Over and over again."

"And you're still not talking to her?"

"I'm never going to talk to her. If I pick up the phone and hear her voice, I just hang up, and if she calls again, either Dad picks it up or I let her talk to the answering machine. Grandma never answers the phone anymore."

"I think you should talk to her."

"I think you should mind your own business."

"My mother thinks so, too."

"And what about Henry? What does he think?"

"You know something?" Laura said. "You're changing, and not in a nice way. I know it's not easy for you, but—"

"You don't know anything," Olivia told her. "And I've got things to do. See you around."

Things to do? What things? Olivia wandered around her room restlessly. Nothing to do in her room. All her homework done except for algebra—and she was so far behind there, she couldn't even remember where she had left off.

Reading? No! TV? No! She opened her door, and walked out into the hall. She paused in front of her father's door, and listened to the usual whirs and clicks and computer voices. She knocked on the door, and Dad called out, "Come in!"

Several of Dad's computers were flashing away, and Dad was sitting in front of two of them, working on a new program he was developing. It was a series that could put you or anyone else into any kind of setting that you chose. Right now, Dad was flashing a group of paintings on each of the two computer screens—on one, a series of portrait paintings from the time when ladies wore flowing, brilliant dresses and plumed hats and, on the other, a series of impressionist paintings. As Olivia moved into the room, Dad quickly pressed a button, and suddenly there were empty spaces where women's faces should have been. Olivia had a pretty good idea whose face had been smiling or frowning under those feathered hats and over those shimmering lacy dresses.

"Uh, Olivia," Dad said guiltily, "uh . . . what's doing?"

"Nothing," Olivia told him.

"How's everything?"

"I'm still failing in algebra," Olivia said, "and I quit the volleyball team, and I'm bored."

"Come here, honey," Dad said, pressing some buttons. "Let me show you something."

Olivia sat next to her father, and suddenly it was her face inside those portrait paintings. There she was: riding a horse; walking through a field of poppies in a long white dress, carrying a parasol; and sitting in a boat with a young man who looked as if he were crazy about her.

"Nope!" Dad said, pressing a button and removing her face from the young man's gaze. "Not yet."

"I liked that one," Olivia said. "Put me back there."

Dad's fingers were moving. "Here's a good one," he said, and there she was with long black hair, her arms around a bundle of calla lilies.

"This is my series of famous paintings," Dad explained. "But I've also developed others—on sculptures, travel, famous historic events. Olivia, your mother called five times today. I want you to talk to her."

"I'm never going to speak to her again," Olivia said. "Can you put my face on the Statue of Liberty?"

"Piece of cake." Dad fiddled around with his keyboard, and there Olivia saw herself, in New York harbor, holding aloft her beacon of light.

"How about one of those yummy statues by . . . what's his name?"

"Rodin," Dad told her. "But Olivia—we can't go on this way. Your mother is miserable, and I know you are, too. And I just can't handle it myself. Oh, wait a minute, wait!"

One of Dad's computers was flashing skulls and crossbones, and Dad hurried to tend to it. Then another screen beeped, and another one burped, and it sounded to Olivia as if another one were barfing. Dad kept moving around the room, pressing buttons, examining screens, and collecting faxes.

"Just a minute, Olivia," Dad said. "We have to talk."

"I'll be in my room," Olivia told him. "We can't talk here."

"I'll be right there," Dad said. "I just need to straighten out a few things, and check my E-mail. I'll be there in five minutes."

Mom called three times, and Olivia hung up three times while she waited for Dad in her room. Then she wandered downstairs and sat with Grandma, who had the TV on but was not looking at it.

"I think I'll go to bed now," Grandma said finally. "Good night, dear."

"Goodnight, Grandma," Olivia said. "I think I'll go to bed, too."

She stuck her head into Dad's room and snarled, "I'm going to bed now, Dad. There's no point in waiting for you."

"But I was just coming in," Dad said. "I told you I needed to straighten out a few things and I'd be right with you."

"That was an hour and a half ago," Olivia told him, "and I'm sick of waiting for you. I'm sick of so many things in my life, I wish I'd never been born. Good night."

Dad jumped up and followed Olivia back into her room.

"I guess I'm not much help to you, am I?" he said. His long, thin face wrinkled mournfully.

No wonder she left him, Olivia thought suddenly, knowing the thought had been there all along. She didn't want to think it, and she struggled to chase it off, but it remained. He's no fun, she thought, and then she caught sight of her own long, mournful face in the mirror. And neither am I. She shut her eyes. No wonder she left the two of us.

"No!" she told Dad. "You're not much help to me, and I guess I'm not much help to you, and nobody's any help to Grandma."

"Okay, but now it's all going to change." Dad sat down next to Olivia and tried to smile naturally. "I've been doing a lot of thinking, and your mother is right. It's time for all of us to move on and forget the past. She's not coming back."

Olivia shrugged. "I wouldn't want her to come back anyway. I can't stand her."

"And, Olivia, you just have to make your peace with

her so we can go on and make some of our own plans."

"I won't."

"Okay—we'll talk about this again when you're a little calmer."

"I'm very calm," Olivia told him. "And I think you should stop being such a jerk. You don't have to be nice to her. She wasn't very nice to you, but you still think about her. I know what you're doing with that new series of yours. I know you're putting her face in all those paintings and sculptures."

Dad didn't say anything.

"Why should you love her so much when she's so rotten to you? At least I have some self-respect. I'm not going to love her when she doesn't care at all for me."

"She does. She does," Dad insisted. "She loves you a lot, Olivia."

"Oh, sure! She's one great mother, isn't she? She thinks she can just walk out on me, and I'll kiss her hand and say, 'Thanks, Mom.' "

"She didn't walk out on you, Olivia. She walked out on me."

"And what about me?" Olivia said, between her teeth. "Wasn't she walking out on me, too?"

"Well," Dad said slowly, "it's not like you're a baby anymore, Olivia. You are growing up."

"Don't give me that," Olivia said furiously. "Even when I was little, she was hardly ever around—not like other people's mothers. Her job always came first, and now, it's Nate and her job."

"Parents are people, too." Dad's face folded up again into its usual mournful folds. "And in a few years, you'll be going away to college and starting a new life, away from her, away from me. She, and I, we have to have other interests in our lives."

"And what about me?" Olivia demanded.

"You need to have other interests, too."

"Like what?"

Dad reached out and gently touched her cheek. "Like . . . like growing up," he said.

Chapter 9

OF COURSE he meant boys, Olivia understood, and, of course, boys were certainly—painfully—among her other interests. At times, it seemed as if boys were her only interest. And not just one boy, either.

Boys unsettled her—sinewy arms under rolled-up sleeves, the new deep sounds of their voices; looking up at the tall ones, down at the short ones. It didn't take much to start her heart pounding or her internal thermostat rising. It was shameful, Olivia thought, to be attracted by so many boys at the same time. All the famous romances celebrated the love of one man and one woman. Olivia found it impossible to keep her mind on only one boy. It was humiliating, and doubly humiliating now, when she was suffering so much because of Mom.

In Spanish she sat behind Jim Morgan, who turned when she clumped into her seat and gave her his crooked smile.

"Did you do the homework, Olive Oyl?" he asked in his most winning voice.

What blue eyes he had! And what gorgeous curly hair!

"Yes," she sighed, smiling, happy that in Spanish at least she was recognized as one of the star students.

"Could I see it for a second? I want to make sure you got it right." His smile grew even more crooked over his straight white teeth. This was not the first time he had copied her homework.

She shook her head but fished the homework out of her folder and handed it to him.

"Thanks!" He bent over his desk, revealing the back of his smooth neck with the silver chain looped around it. Her heart began thumping so hard she could hear it up in her ears, and that embarrassing, warm feeling spread out inside her.

Cute Catholic boys who wore medals on silver chains around their necks were particularly unsettling. She tried to keep her eyes on the front of the classroom where Señora Alvarez was writing on the blackboard, but they kept returning to the smooth brown neck in front of her. Catholic boys were forbidden. Olivia could hear Grandma's voice, from the days before Grandpa died, issuing the injunction: "Only Jewish boys! You have to keep to your own!"

Maybe so, but Olivia could still safely daydream. Nobody could look inside her head while she and Jim Morgan walked hand in hand on the beach or curled up together, very close, on a hill covered with poppies.

If he were the only one, it would be bad enough, but in algebra, there was Ron Kramer (at least he was Jewish) and in English, Jason Rhodes (who wasn't). And so many others as well—just bumping into somebody in the hall, a stranger, was enough to start the fires burning.

"I wasn't like this before my bat mitzvah," Olivia confessed to Laura. "I didn't even like boys then."

"I always liked them," Laura said, "but they never liked me."

They were eating their lunch outside, above the football field, and watching the couples.

"There's Katie Carpenter with Fred Thompson. I thought she was going around with Nick Chu."

"She's always got some guy interested in her." They watched as Katie laughed and pushed Fred, who laughed and pushed her back.

"What is it about her?" Olivia asked. "Why do boys like her so much?"

"Well, she's pretty," Laura said, "and she knows how to talk to boys."

"I wonder," Olivia said, "I wonder if I'll ever learn how."

In algebra, while she was pretending to check the clock on the side wall but was really looking at Ron Kramer, Mr. Harper began returning the last test papers. Mr. Harper was one of the nastiest teachers in the school, and whenever he returned test papers, he relished announcing each student's mark.

"One hundred percent." Mr. Harper nodded approvingly at Lisa Ng. "Not the first time for Lisa, either, is it? And certainly not the last." He handed Lisa her paper.

"Ninety-eight percent—Ron Kramer," Mr. Harper said with another approving nod. "You've been slipping a little, my boy. Ninety-eight—Rose Lister. No surprises there. Ninety-seven—Ryan James . . ."

That last test had not been a total mystery to Olivia, as some of the others had been, and she looked hopefully at each paper Mr. Harper held up.

"Eighty-three percent—Shannon Means, eighty—Lester Singh . . ."

She remained hopeful as the numbers moved down into the seventies and the sixties, and then forgot all about boys and all about her mother as the numbers continued dipping. Finally, Mr. Harper held up the last paper, scowling, and narrowing his eyes. "Thirty percent," he said, "Olivia Diamond. Thirty percent," he repeated, shaking his head.

Some kids tittered, and Olivia felt hot and cold at the same time. "It will certainly take a miracle, I would say, for you to pass this course, Olivia."

My life is totally in shambles, Olivia was thinking as she hurried along the hall after class, the sound of her classmates laughter still in her ears. She had never failed anything in her whole life, and now she was certain to fail algebra. Panic panted and snarled at her heels, and she speeded up to escape from it.

"Olivia! Olivia!" somebody was calling. "Wait up, Olivia!"

And there was Ron Kramer hurrying to catch up.

And there he stood, smiling down at her sympathetically.

"Harper's a creep," he said. "Don't let him get to you."

She shrugged, and tried to think of something clever to say.

"Where are you going now?" Ron asked.

"Uh—to English."

"With Baxter?"

"Uh—yes."

"That's up the hall, right?"

He fell in step beside her, and since her English class was only four classrooms down the hall, they didn't have very far to go, and she didn't have much time to think of anything else to say.

"Look—I've been tutoring some kids—privately, I mean—and I just wondered if you'd be interested."

"Interested?" Olivia repeated, looking up at his dark blond hair and yellow-green eyes.

"Well—I'm charging ten dollars an hour. That's pretty cheap. Most tutors charge twenty-five dollars, but since I'm only fifteen and just starting out, I think it's fair. I wondered if you'd be interested."

"Oh, yes," Olivia said quickly. "I'm interested."

Ron grinned and fished around in his pocket. "Here, I even made up a card. It has my phone number on it. I could come to your house, but then I would have to charge an extra five dollars if I did. Or you could come to mine. Where do you live?"

"On Thirty-eighth, near Fulton."

"Well, I'm over on Anza and Thirty-fifth, so it's just a short walk."

The bell rang.

"Why don't you give me a ring when you decide. I'm sure I can help you."

"Okay, I will—I mean—yes, I will."

"Great! I've got to run." He smiled and touched her arm. Olivia stood there watching him sprint down the hall. Then she looked down at the card in her hand. *Ron Kramer*, it said. *Tutoring in math and chemistry.*

Chapter 10

COME OUT for a walk, Grandma," Olivia offered generously. "It's such a beautiful day. We can go to Spreckels Lake if you like."

Grandma was wearing her pale peach raw-silk suit with the coordinated peach-and-blue ruffly blouse that she had worn to Olivia's bat mitzvah.

"That sounds nice, dear," Grandma said, slowly rising. "I'll just get my coat."

"Maybe you should put something else on, Grandma. You look lovely, but maybe it's a little dressy for Spreckels Lake."

"I'll be right back," Grandma said.

Dad had left a note on the kitchen table, saying he was meeting with somebody who was interested in a couple of his art programs and wouldn't be back until later. He was expecting to work out a deal and would take them all out to dinner if he did—and even if he didn't.

Grandma returned, still in her peach suit, with a pale blue coat. She looked as if she were going to a party, but Olivia restrained herself.

"Dad says he's expecting to sell some of his programs, and that he'll take us all out to dinner."

"That's nice," Grandma said vaguely. She held Olivia's arm lightly as they crossed Fulton. Olivia remembered how Grandma had always gripped her arm whenever they crossed any street and how she had always urged her to look both ways before crossing. Grandma was looking straight ahead.

"You know, Grandma, I've been feeling pretty miserable, too. Not only for Grandpa. I miss him very much, but for Mom—for my mother."

Grandma shook her head, and then she sniffed the air. "It smells so good here," she said.

"But today something nice happened. I failed my algebra test. I got only thirty percent." Suddenly Olivia began laughing.

Grandma smiled. "That's nice," she said.

"No, Grandma, it wasn't nice. But then, this boy came up and offered to tutor me. His name is Ron Kramer."

"I know his grandmother," Grandma said. She and Olivia were passing a group of men on one of the long benches, playing dominoes.

"How do you know that you know his grandmother?" Olivia asked, startled.

"Ruth Kramer," Grandma recited. "Her boy, David, and your father were friends. David has two sons—Ron and Jeff. They live over on Thirty-fifth or Thirty-fourth. David came to Grandpa's funeral. So did Ruth."

"Grandma, that's wonderful. I mean, sometimes you seem so—so out of it."

Grandma paused at the new big turtle statue in the lake, with all the real, live turtles sitting on its back. "That statue wasn't here when Grandpa and I walked around the lake. He never saw that statue."

"I guess—I guess you loved him very much, Grandma," Olivia said. She had a picture in her mind of Grandpa—short, paunchy Grandpa with a large, dark mole on one of his cheeks.

"I did," Grandma said, still looking at the turtle statue. "I do."

"Well, but Grandma, you must have known other boys—I mean when you were young. You must have liked other boys."

"No," Grandma said. "Only him. I loved him right away. He's the only man I ever loved, the only man I ever could have loved."

"Well, Grandma, do you feel it's not natural to like different boys—not only one, like you did."

"I only loved him," Grandma said. "He was the only one."

She started walking again, and Olivia wondered if Ron Kramer would turn out to be the only one for her. After all, she hadn't ever really done more than notice other boys and maybe do a little harmless daydreaming.

Grandma paused now in front of the side of the lake where the men—it was only men—sailed their model boats. A bunch of boats were out this afternoon—radio operated model boats, each one different from the other. There was a cargo boat with a load of coal, a freighter, a tugboat, and a little fireboat called the *Mary S.* It had a crew and tiny little hoses to put out fires on ships at sea.

"Look, Grandma, aren't they darling! And Grandma,

look at that little fireboat. It's heading back to the shore. Look, Grandma, it's coming straight toward us."

But Grandma seemed to have lost interest and was looking across the water at an empty spot on the path.

The model fireboat came closer and closer, and Olivia could see the three members of the crew, all holding tiny hoses.

"Oh, Grandma, just look at them. They're so cute—Grandma—oh, no!"

All of the tiny hoses suddenly spurted out water, not at a ship on fire but on Grandma's beautiful peach raw-silk skirt. Olivia put out her hand, but it was too late, and three sprays of dirty water began flowering out on the pale peach material. She heard laughter, like the laughter in her algebra class that morning, and looked up angrily at a clump of old men, sitting over their controls, laughing and pretending to be looking in the other direction.

"That's not funny," Olivia shouted, grabbing Grandma's hand and moving closer to confront them. The tittering continued, and one man elbowed another, who was laughing louder than his companions.

"Just look at what you did to my grandmother's dress. Just look!"

The laughing man turned to face them. "Aw—it's just a little spray. It'll dry up. Can't you take a joke?"

"Sure I can take a joke, but if it was your grandmother, I bet you wouldn't think it was funny."

The other men were smirking now, and Olivia shouted at all of them, "You should be ashamed of yourselves. You're acting like a bunch of kids."

"Olivia," said her grandmother. "It's all right, Olivia. I'm fine."

The laughing man, not laughing now but smiling, put down his radio, stood up, and approached them.

"I'm sorry, lady," he said to Grandma, "but you sure are lucky to have a granddaughter who sticks up for you like that."

"Yes," Grandma said. "I'm very lucky."

Olivia dug some tissues out of her pocket, and began dabbing at Grandma's skirt. The spray was drying, but on the pale peach material small but noticeable dirty stains remained.

"Look what you did," she said over her shoulder to the man. "You ruined my grandmother's dress. She'll never be able to get the stains off."

"Well, I'll be willing to pay for dry cleaning," said the

man, in what sounded like a cranky voice. "I'm always here on Thursday afternoons and Saturday mornings. Sometimes on Wednesday afternoons, too. If you want to show me the cleaning bill, I'll pay for it—I mean, if it's reasonable."

"No!" Grandma said. "No! No cleaning bill. It's all right, Olivia."

"Well, thank you, lady," the man said. "You're a good sport, and I'm sorry. What else can I say?"

"Nothing," Grandma said. "It was a joke. Come on, Olivia."

She took Olivia's arm and pulled her away. Olivia threw a dirty look at the man, and then she said to Grandma as they walked off, "You should have let him pay for the dry cleaning. I don't even know if they can dry-clean it. It's probably ruined."

"It's only a skirt," Grandma said.

"Well, I did say maybe you should wear something else," Olivia pointed out. "I thought it was too dressy for Spreckels Lake."

"I think I'll sit down," Grandma said, "but you go on with your walk, Olivia."

"No, I'll sit down, too," Olivia said. She tried to start the conversation up again about the blotches on

Grandma's skirt, but it became evident that Grandma was no longer listening. Grandma was looking off—not at an empty spot on the path but back to where the knot of old men were sitting, sailing their boats.

Chapter
11

OLIVIA SETTLED with Ron Kramer that she would come to his house on Wednesday afternoons from four to five.

"That's a good day," Ron said over the phone. "I only have one other student."

"What should I bring?" Olivia asked.

"Just your brain," Ron told her, laughing. "If you have one."

Olivia did not think that remark particularly funny, but she gave an uneasy chuckle before she hung up.

Wednesday, before leaving for Ron's house, she brushed her hair back into a ponytail and tied it with a bright red tie. Then she pulled on a red T-shirt that said CHICKEN LICKEN on it and showed a huge chicken licking a tiny man. She checked herself in the mirror. Nope! She pulled off the T-shirt and the ponytail tie. Then she put on her black 49ers T-shirt and let her hair hang down loose. Nope! That didn't look right either. She ended up wearing a plain pink T-shirt and black jeans, with her hair in a French braid. She spun around slowly in front of the mirror, examining herself front, sides, and as much back as she could see. Too bad she wasn't thinner and shorter, with a smaller nose, larger eyes, and fuller mouth, like Mom. But her skin was pretty good, and when she smiled, she had two dimples in her cheeks. She wondered if Ron thought she was pretty. She wondered what else he thought about her.

On the way over, she tried to remember if there had ever been a time when she understood algebra.

Olivia arranged herself in front of his door and rang the bell. As soon as Ron opened it, she leaped into his arms and wrapped her arms around him.

"Whu—what?" Ron managed to say.

"Get him away! Get him away!" Olivia shrieked. The dog was jumping up on her and licking any part it could reach.

"It's only Lulu," Ron said, trying to disentangle himself. "Just calm down."

"I'll wait outside," Olivia yelled, running back out the door. "Put him in another room. I'll wait outside."

She pulled the door closed behind her and stood on the steps, almost frozen in terror.

After a while, Ron opened the door, grinning. "Okay, it's safe now. You can come in."

"Where's the dog?" Olivia asked. Her voice sounded shrill and silly even to herself.

"She's out in the yard. You're really something. Nobody's ever afraid of Lulu. It's always the other way around. She's afraid of her own shadow, but she certainly seemed to like you."

"Lulu?"

"The dog. She's a miniature French poodle. Boy!" He was grinning again. "If I thought she had that effect on all girls, I'd always bring her to the door with me."

"I'm really sorry," Olivia told him. "I just have this fear of dogs, because when I was three, a big dog chased me and bit me, and I never got over it." Olivia tried to explain how she had tried to get the better of it, but the memory of that big dog out of her childhood memories just would not go away. She was describing Laura's dog,

Henry, when she noticed that Ron was checking his watch.

"It's nearly a quarter after four," he said. "I have another student coming at five, so we'd better get started."

Olivia moved cautiously into the house. "You're sure the dog can't get out?"

"Okay. Here, take a look." He led her over to a window that overlooked the backyard. She looked down, and there was Lulu looking up. Lulu's tail began wagging, and she barked and ran up the back stairs.

"Oh! Oh!" Olivia cried. "She's coming up the stairs. She's—"

"The door's locked," Ron told her impatiently. "Besides, we always keep her in the backyard. It was just that the painter was repairing some of the plaster on the back wall, and Lulu was making a racket so we brought her inside. Otherwise, she's out all day and sometimes all night if we forget to bring her in. Anyway, let's go into the dining room and get started. We're wasting time."

"I think the best way to start," Ron said, once they were settled at the dining-room table, "is to review some of the algebraic terms so you know what we're talking about. Okay?"

"Okay," Olivia agreed. Maybe algebra would turn out

to be easy once a good teacher, like Ron, got her off to a good start.

But almost as soon as Ron began talking about co-efficients, linear equations, and variables—very slowly and clearly, and pausing every so often with an encouraging smile—she had to admit she still found herself helplessly confused.

"Okay?" he kept asking.

"Uh, okay," she found herself agreeing, even though it wasn't okay.

Why wasn't it? she wondered. None of her other classes had ever baffled her in the same way. But algebra with its x's, y's, and z's didn't make any sense at all, didn't relate to anything that mattered in her life, even though Ron was explaining how algebraic equations did apply to everyday life.

The only application to her life she could find was Ron himself. She could see he must be an excellent teacher even though she could not understand anything he was telling her.

"Okay?"

"Okay."

She tried to look intelligent, nodding thoughtfully every so often and agreeing when Ron said he could see she could catch on very quickly. It wasn't only that he was so good looking, but also she loved his enthusiasm—his obvious pleasure in algebra. It was exciting when a person felt passionate about something, the way Mom always felt about her work or the people she knew. Well, what did she, Olivia, feel passionate about, she wondered?

"I'm sorry to interrupt, but, Ron, your coach is on the phone. He needs to talk to you right now," said Ron's mother, standing in the doorway.

"I'll be back in a second, Olivia. Why don't you just look over these problems? We'll do some of them next."

But Mrs. Kramer came into the room after Ron left and said in a low voice to Olivia, "The coach calls him all the time."

"Who?"

"The coach—from the tennis team—Mr. Stoyanoff. Ron is captain of the team, and the coach is always asking his advice." Mrs. Kramer shook her head. "He thinks Ron is good enough to be a pro, but, naturally, he's going into some kind of science. Ron's just an exceptional person, good in everything."

No wonder she's so proud of him, Olivia thought when she'd gone. Why wouldn't she be? She looked down at the book in front of her, and nothing made any sense at all. She could also hear the dog barking from the yard, feeding into the panic which was beginning to grow inside her.

"Okay now," Ron said, sitting down in his chair. "Now let's do some of these problems. I'm sure you won't have any trouble understanding them."

On the way home, Olivia had to acknowledge that the lesson had been pretty much a bust. She had not been able to understand any of the problems, and she could see that Ron was disappointed, even though he continued to smile and say "Okay?" Then the next student, also a girl, came five minutes early and sat in the living room so that Ron had to hurriedly finish Olivia's lesson.

"Maybe you ought to come twice a week for a while," he suggested, "if you want to pass. You seem to have gotten off to a bad start, and I think we should just go back and start all over again from the beginning."

That was the only good thing that had come out of the whole lesson. You have to get a grip on yourself, Olivia told herself severely. He obviously thinks you're pretty stupid, and then you're terrified of his dog. He's probably crazy about that dog the way Laura and Todd are about Henry. And then the way you threw yourself on him! Olivia's neck and ears burned with shame. It was disgusting. You might as well forget all about him. How could he ever care for somebody like you?

But Olivia decided she would take two lessons a week from Ron, starting immediately.

Chapter
12

IN BETWEEN lessons, Olivia daydreamed about Ron. She hardly paid any attention to Jim Morgan's neck in Spanish, although she let him copy her Spanish homework whenever he asked, and she didn't even notice that Jason Rhodes had been absent about a whole week in English.

Ron was even better looking than she had originally noticed. His thick golden brown hair lay like a gleaming mane on his head. He had a way of tossing it, and she loved to watch it rise up into the air and fall back perfectly in place again. She also loved the way he looked at her very seriously as he explained the mysteries of algebra.

"Just remember that coefficients are the number parts of each term. It's really a snap. For instance, the coefficient of $-6x$ is -6, and the coefficient of $2y$ is 2. Nothing complicated about that. Okay?"

Olivia struggled to understand. It was uncomfortable and humiliating not being able to comprehend something that other people found easy. She knew she was intelligent. In almost all of her other subjects, she was the one who knew more than the other students. But Ron was only in her algebra class. What could he think of her?

Sometimes she thought he liked her. Sometimes his yellow-green eyes lingered on her, and sometimes he laughed at her when she stood hesitantly at his door before coming inside to make certain that Lulu was outside. And every time the lesson ended, he walked her to the door, saying he thought she was making progress— even though she knew she was not—and always patted her arm before saying, "See you soon."

The rainy season began with a bang in the middle of October. Even though she wore her slicker and carried an umbrella, Olivia was drenched by the time she reached Ron's house.

"Come in, come in!" Ron urged. He took her umbrella and opened it up in the small vestibule between the inside of the house and the outside. Then he took her slicker and hung it up on the clothes rack.

"Your shoes are soaked," he said. "Why don't you take them off, and I'll lend you a pair of my socks."

"Oh, no!" Olivia mumbled. "It's okay—really!"

"Listen, you just take off your shoes and socks while I run upstairs."

"No, really!"

"Come on, Olivia. I can't afford to lose my best student, can I?" he said, grinning. "Here, sit on this bench. I'll be right back."

In a few minutes, she was wearing Ron's socks—a wonderful thick pair of gray socks—while her shoes and socks were drying off in front of a heater in the hall.

"Let's have a cup of cocoa or tea or whatever you like," he offered.

"No, honestly, I'm fine." And she was, wriggling her toes deliciously inside his socks.

"Well, I'm going to make me a cup of cocoa, and I'll make you one, too. Why don't you look over the homework, and—"

Suddenly Olivia heard barking and jumped up. "Where is the dog?" she cried.

Ron said, grinning, "Out in the backyard, of course. I'll be right back."

While he was gone, Olivia moved cautiously over to the window. It was pouring buckets outside, and a very wet, very miserable little dog was standing on the back steps, whining. When she noticed Olivia watching from the window, her tail began wagging, and Olivia couldn't help noticing how the rain was plastering down the fur on her head. She followed Ron into the kitchen. He was busy stirring the cocoa, and the whole room felt wonderfully warm and cozy.

"Ron, look, I really wouldn't mind if Lulu was indoors as long as she wasn't in the same room with me."

Ron began pouring the cocoa into two mugs. "It's okay," he said, "she doesn't mind the rain. She can always get under the back steps. It's dry there." He held out a mug of cocoa to her. "Let's take it back into the dining room."

The cocoa smelled wonderful and felt wonderful as it went down. Lulu kept barking, and Olivia set down her mug.

"I think you should let Lulu come inside," she said bravely to Ron. "It's such a terrible day. Honestly, if she stayed in the kitchen, it wouldn't bother me at all."

Ron opened his algebra book. "She's used to it," he said impatiently. "Most of the time she's out in the back-yard anyway. None of us want to put up with her. She's really a pain in the neck, to tell you the truth. Jeff, my brother, always thought he wanted a dog, but it didn't take long for him to realize it was too much trouble tak-ing care of one. Now that he's on the swim team at school, he's hardly ever home."

"I thought Lulu was your dog."

"I can't stand her," Ron said. "She's really dumb. Any-way, let's get started. Did you try to do any of the home-work yet?"

Laura was incredulous. "You mean he left that poor dog out in the yard all the time you were there?"

"Well, I told him he could let her in, but he said she's used to it and that she could always go under the steps if she wanted to get out of the rain. He also said she was pretty stupid and that he couldn't stand her."

"And you like this guy?"

Olivia said tenderly, "He loaned me his socks. He made me take my shoes and socks off, and he loaned me his socks, and he made me cocoa, and then he asked his mother to drive me home because it was still pouring."

"But he left the dog outside?"

"Well, maybe she is used to it. His mother didn't bring her inside, either."

"Nice family," Laura said.

"I think he's beginning to like me," Olivia confided. "He really seemed upset that I got so wet."

"Big deal!"

"Anyway, Laura, tomorrow's Thursday. How about getting together?"

"I have my violin lesson on Thursdays."

"That's right. When are you going to tell your father you're giving up the violin?"

"Let's get together Friday," Laura said. "As a matter of fact, come for dinner and sleep over. Just give me an hour or so to practice. Come around five, and we can hang out most of Saturday. I decided not to tell my father."

"But I thought you had definitely decided you would tell him."

"I guess I thought I had, but I can't do it. I think he'd be devastated. Especially now that my teacher thinks I'm ready."

"Ready? For what?"

"Well, he thinks I should try out for the city youth orchestra. And he also thinks I should transfer to the High School of Music and Art."

"But that's crazy, Laura. You don't want to, do you?"
Laura remained silent.

"Listen, Laura," Olivia said, "you can't live your life just to make your father happy. Parents don't worry about our happiness when they want to do something. You have to live your own life, and if you want to give up music, go ahead and give it up."

"I don't know," Laura said glumly. "I just don't know."

"But you were so sure."

"Now I'm not. I'm not sure about lots of things. Are you always sure?"

"I'm sure about my mother," said Olivia. "She makes me feel bad whenever I see her, and I don't want to see her anymore. And if your father is making you do something you don't want to do, just stop doing it."

"But that's just it," Laura said. "He is, and he isn't. I mean I felt really happy when my teacher said I should try out for the youth orchestra, and I felt proud when he said I should transfer to Music and Art. You know, Olivia, the best thing I do is play the violin. I know that. I've always known it—and I also know I could even play better if I stopped worrying about my father and concentrated on getting rid of my stupid stage fright."

Olivia said slowly, "If you transferred to Music and Art, I wouldn't see much of you."

"Oh, sure you would," Laura insisted.

"No, I wouldn't," Olivia said. "I never see much of you as it is nowadays, because you're always practicing. But at least I see you every day in school for lunch and sometimes over the weekends. But if you go to Music and Art, you'll meet other kids into music like you, and I'll never see you."

"We'll always be best friends," Laura said stubbornly. "And I haven't really decided yet if I am going to transfer. So let's just forget about it. Anyway, how about sleeping over tomorrow night? And Saturday—well, if it stops raining, we could bike over to the beach. And if it rains—well, we could go to the movies or whatever you like. Okay, Olivia?"

"Okay," Olivia agreed helplessly, feeling another part of her life slipping away.

Chapter

13

MOM WAS waiting for her after school on Monday. Olivia and Laura were halfway down the steps when Laura said, "Oh, hi, Mrs. Diamond."

"Hi, Laura," Mom said, smiling uncertainly and looking at Olivia.

Olivia didn't say anything. "Hi, Olivia," Mom said. Olivia did not answer.

"Olivia," Laura said, "your mother is talking to you."

"I heard her," Olivia said. "Come on, Laura, I need to get home."

But before she could move, someone ran down the steps behind her. "Olivia, wait a minute!" It was Ron. "I just remembered that I won't be able to give you your lesson tomorrow." He made a face. "I forgot—I have to go to the dentist."

He smiled at Olivia. Then he smiled at Laura, and then he smiled at Mom.

"This is my friend, Laura Franklin," Olivia mumbled. "Laura—Ron Kramer."

"And this is Mrs. Diamond, Olivia's mother," Laura added.

"Hi, Mrs. Diamond," Ron said. "I think we'll make an astrophysicist out of your daughter one of these days."

"Ron is tutoring Olivia in algebra," Laura explained.

"You study violin with Mr. Hooper, don't you?" Ron asked, turning to Laura.

"Uh-huh. How did you know?"

Ron grinned. "Well, my friend, Alan Hammer, also takes lessons with him."

"Oh sure. I know Alan. He's pretty good."

"Well, he thinks you're great—and not only your playing, either. Anyway, Olivia, how about changing your Tuesday lesson to Thursday or Friday. Are you free?"

"I guess so. Maybe Thursday would be better."

"Fine. I'll see you then. Nice meeting you, Mrs. Diamond. Laura."

"I wonder what he meant," Laura said, looking after Ron's back.

"He meant he couldn't give me a lesson tomorrow. I have to come Thursday."

"No. I mean about Alan Hammer."

"Who?"

"He meant," Mom said, smiling, "that his friend, Alan Hammer, who also studies with your violin teacher, thinks that you're not only a marvelous player, but that you're a marvelous girl as well."

"Oh, Mrs. Diamond! Anyway . . ." Laura suddenly stopped grinning foolishly and began backing away. "I guess the two of you want a little time by yourselves."

"No, we don't," Olivia said.

"So I'll be going. Nice seeing you, Mrs. Diamond!" Laura leaped down the steps and practically flew off along the street.

Olivia turned her face away from Mom and pretended to be absorbed in watching Laura.

"Olivia," came her mother's voice, "let's go somewhere, just the two of us, and talk."

Olivia shook her head and continued watching Laura hurry along the street. She could hear Mom's breathing as she moved closer, and then, Mom put a hand on her head and began stroking her hair. "You've gotten a hair-cut," she said. "It looks . . ."

"I went to Super Shears, and it only cost six dollars," Olivia said angrily. "And if you don't like it, that's just too bad."

"No! No!" Mom said, dropping her arm until it rested around Olivia's shoulder. It actually looks very . . . very interesting. It gives you a kind of pixie look."

Olivia shrugged. She wanted to push Mom's arm away and run, but it felt so good, feeling Mom's arm around her and smelling Mom's warm, fresh smell.

"That was a very nice boy, that Rod," Mom said.

"Ron!" Olivia corrected, still looking away.

Mom moved closer. Now she had one arm around Olivia's shoulder, and she suddenly reached her other arm across and took Olivia's hand.

"I have to go," Olivia said weakly.

"I thought we could have a snack someplace, like that little pastry shop on Twenty-third. Would you like that, darling?"

"I'm not hungry," Olivia lied.

"Well, I am," Mom said. "I didn't have any lunch—just a couple of carrot sticks and some peanuts. You remember that double chocolate brownie they make? I know you've always been crazy about that brownie, and so am I. Let's go there."

"I think I'm cooking tonight. I should go home," Olivia said weakly as her mother led her down the stairs.

"Oh, that's right," said Mom. "How is your grandmother?"

"About the same."

Mom opened the door of her car and eased Olivia into the passenger seat. "She needs to see a psychiatrist," Mom said. "Maybe get on one of those antidepressants."

"That's what Uncle Dan says." Olivia leaned back and felt the leather seat in the car and breathed the leather smell. Mom drove a little sport car, and she'd forgotten how important it always made her feel when she drove with Mom. Dad drove a Plymouth.

"Well, isn't this fun?" Mom said when they were seated at one of the little tables in the cafe, their brownies and drinks in front of them. "It feels like old times, doesn't it, darling?"

Olivia raised her eyes from the brownie and, for the first time, looked directly at Mom. "No," she said, "it doesn't feel like old times, because you've gone away. You've gone away and left us."

"No, Olivia, I have not left you. I'll never leave you,

and"—Mom laughed suddenly—"and I won't let you leave me, either. You're my child, my precious one and only child."

"But now you have Beth and Alison. You don't need me anymore."

Mom shook her head, smiled, and leaned over closer. "You're my one and only, Olivia. You'll always be my one and only. Beth and Alison are darling girls, and I do love them. But Olivia, you are my daughter. Let's not make any mistake about that. Okay?"

Suddenly it felt as if she were sitting there with Ron, trying to make sense of algebra. She shook her head but began eating her brownie.

"Well, now that we've got that settled," Mom said, leaning back, "I want to ask you about Rod."

"Ron."

"Yes, Ron. How come he's tutoring you in algebra?"

And then, to her amazement, Olivia began talking. She talked about Ron, and how she could not understand algebra at all, even with Ron tutoring her. She told Mom about Mr. Harper and how he had humiliated her. She told Mom how she had quit volleyball, and then she told her about Laura's plans and how everything was changing in her life—all for the worse.

"Everything changes in life," Mom said, putting a second brownie on Olivia's plate. "Often for the better."

"Not for me," Olivia said, beginning to eat the second brownie.

"Yes, for you, too," said Mom. "And once you accept changes, you'll find—"

Olivia interrupted her. "Do you really think Ron's friend is interested in Laura?"

"It certainly sounds that way."

Olivia tried to smile, but she could feel the waves of jealousy rising inside her. Laura's life was certainly changing for the better. She would become a musician, her father would be happy and proud, Alan Hammer would take her to the junior and senior prom, while she, Olivia . . .

"I don't think Ron is interested in me," Olivia said.

"Oh, I don't know about that. He certainly seemed friendly."

But Olivia shook her head. Suddenly the brownie didn't taste good anymore, and she pushed it away.

Chapter
14

EARLY IN November, Grandma cooked her first Shabbat dinner since Grandpa died.

"The matzo balls need more salt," she said, "and the soup has no taste. They didn't have any fresh dill at the market."

"It's just wonderful, Mama," Aunt Ellen said, "and I'll have another matzo ball if you have any extra."

Grandma wore an apron over an everyday dress and didn't look at the door even once.

"What happened?" Aunt Ellen asked Dad while Grandma was in the kitchen, dishing out the fruit compote. "Last week she was still almost comatose."

"No, she wasn't," Olivia said. "She's been taking walks by herself lately, and last week she told Dad he spends too much time with his computers and should get out more."

"I didn't know that." Aunt Ellen grinned at Dad. "Of course she's right."

But Dad didn't grin back. He shook his head impatiently. Then he stood up and began carrying the dishes and silverware back to the kitchen.

"He really should get out more," Aunt Ellen whispered to Olivia when Dad was out of the room. "But I can't get over your grandmother. It's almost like old times."

But it wasn't like old times. When Grandpa was alive, Grandma mostly talked about her family, or about activities at the temple, or about Grandpa's business. She also talked about the weather, the way everybody talks about the weather. But now she talked about it as if it really were important. When the weather was sunny, Grandma seemed particularly cheerful. When it was rainy, she appeared restless and sullen. On sunny afternoons lately, when Olivia returned from school, Grandma was out and did not return until dark.

"Where did you go, Grandma?" Olivia always asked.

"Oh—just out and around," Grandma said evasively.

"Were you visiting one of your friends?"

"No—I was just out."

Grandma's color improved, and she got a haircut. She also bought herself some pants and sweatshirts. One day, Grandma remarked angrily that she'd been asked to sign a stupid petition down at Spreckels Lake.

"Oh?" Olivia said. "What kind of a petition?"

"Some crank tried to say that the little model powerboats were injuring the ducks, and he wanted them prohibited from the lake."

Olivia suddenly grew suspicious. They were eating dinner, and she looked meaningfully at Dad. As usual, he seemed off in the clouds somewhere and wasn't really listening.

"I told him off," Grandma continued.

"What did you tell him?" Olivia asked, baiting the trap.

"I told him this is a free country, and people who build model boats have as much right to sail them in the lake as the ducks have to swim there. And that, in my opinion, any normal duck should have enough sense to get out of the way."

"So you didn't sign?"

"Of course not."

"Did anybody sign?"

"Maybe a few. But most of the people down at Spreckels Lake love the little boats—maybe more than they love the ducks, or the pigeons, who really mess up the place."

"I suppose all those nasty old men who were laughing when you got your dress sprayed—I guess they didn't sign?"

But Grandma was too smart to walk into that one and did not answer.

So Thursday, when Dad was in his room, absorbed in his clicking, flashing, buzzing computers, Olivia walked over to Spreckels Lake by herself. The day was sunny and clear, and the lake's population had swelled. Young couples sprawled on the grassy slopes; babies toddled along, chased by their parents; the benches were filled with men playing chess or dominoes and women talking to one another. The little hot-dog cart was doing a brisk business, Olivia noticed, even though it was four o'clock in the afternoon.

And Grandma sat, laughing, inside the clump of old men sailing their model boats.

It was not that Olivia wanted Grandma to remain unhappy or that she begrudged her any new interests. But Grandma had always been Grandma, with the kind of interests appropriate to anybody's grandmother. Aunt Ellen tried to get Grandma to take some courses, which was appropriate, and Uncle Dan had even suggested a trip, maybe a tour with other seniors, which was also appropriate.

And then Grandma had insisted—just a few weeks ago—that Grandpa was the only man she had ever loved, which was also appropriate for a grandmother.

Olivia lay in wait for Grandma, and when she returned that afternoon, said, "You look a little sunburned, Grandma. Where did you go today?"

"Here and there," Grandma said.

"Maybe down to Spreckels Lake?" Olivia suggested.

"Maybe." Grandma cocked her head, and raised her eyebrows. "I thought I saw you standing there this afternoon. I even said to John, 'I think I see my granddaughter.' Why didn't you come over?"

"John? Is that his name?"

"Yes," Grandma said. "His name is John Cheney. And I still don't know why you didn't come over and say hello."

"Well, to tell you the truth, Grandma," Olivia said, "you haven't been exactly anxious to tell us about your new friends. I wasn't sure you'd be glad to see me."

"Sit down, Olivia," Grandma said, leading her into the living room.

"I have to cook tonight," Olivia said.

"Pizza again?"

"Well, yes."

"That won't take long. I'll help you."

Grandma's face was sunburned, particularly her nose. Her hair stood up in windblown wisps. In the past, Grandma always went to the beauty parlor once a week and wore her hair in a carefully arranged style.

"I think I'm beginning to feel like myself," Grandma said.

"You don't look like yourself," Olivia told her.

"Maybe not." Grandma smiled. "But I feel like myself again."

"I'm happy for you," Olivia said in a sulky voice.

"Are you, Olivia? You don't sound very happy."

Olivia knew that she could not explain to Grandma what she really felt. For thirteen years, nothing had changed in her life. And now, in this past year, everything had changed, and was continuing to change—even Grandma.

"You know, Olivia, you're a young girl, and—"

"Please, Grandma, don't start in about how young I am and how I can't understand. Mom did that to me all the time when she left Dad, and I couldn't stand it."

"No. I wasn't going to say you couldn't understand. I was going to say you are a young girl, and you have your life in front of you. I'm an old woman, and most of my life has gone."

"You're not so old, Grandma. You're only sixty-nine, and Laura's great-grandmother—she's ninety, and she still drives and goes on trips."

Grandma wasn't listening. "When Grandpa died, I thought my life was all over."

"I know, Grandma. I know. And really, you don't have to tell me anything. If you're feeling better, I'm glad."

"I thought I had nothing else to live for. My children were grown up. They had their own families. Maybe they had some problems, too, but there wasn't anything I could do to help. What else was there for me to live for?"

"Please, Grandma, please!" Olivia didn't want to hear anything more. She felt ashamed of herself for baiting Grandma and terrified at what Grandma might tell her.

"So I just sat around and waited. Maybe I should have taken one of those antidepressants like that doctor said, but I didn't. I just waited." She took Olivia's hand and held it.

"I'm sorry, Grandma," Olivia said. "I didn't mean to make you feel bad. I'm happy you're feeling better."

Grandma pressed Olivia's hand. "There was something Grandpa used to say whenever I felt down. Even when we were hiding from the Nazis—even then—when I felt sometimes like just giving up and not struggling anymore. 'Wait!' He used to say. 'Just wait! One day everything is terrible, and you think you can't go on. But then, another day comes along, and it all changes.' Oh, he was a smart man, your grandfather!"

"Do you miss him, Grandma? Still?"

"Of course I miss him," Grandma said. "I'll always miss him. But he was right. One day, I was ready to die, and then, suddenly, there came another day, and everything changed. I was alive again—just like that." She smiled at Olivia. "You think because you've lived a long time that life doesn't have any more surprises for you, but it does. It always does."

"It sure does," Olivia agreed grimly. "Just look at how my mother walked out on us."

Grandma nodded. "So many bad things happen to us we forget that good things can happen, too. For all of us." She pressed Olivia's hand. "You're a good girl, Olivia, and there will be plenty of good surprises in store for you, too. In the meantime, I want you to know that you're wrong about John. He's not a nasty old man—he's a wonderful person."

"Well, he did mess up your dress, and he did laugh and think it was funny."

"He lost his wife three years ago," Grandma said, "and his children both live in the East. He volunteers two days a week at the San Francisco General Hospital in the cancer ward, and the rest of the time he builds his boats and sails them. It keeps him happy."

"That's nice, Grandma. I guess he's a good man if you say so."

"He loves children. He has two grandsons, but he only sees them once or twice a year because they live in the East, too. He thought you were wonderful because of the way you stood up for me."

Olivia hesitated. "Is he Jewish, Grandma?"

"No, he's not."

"But you always told me I shouldn't ever go out with somebody who isn't Jewish."

"I'm not going out with him, Olivia. He's just a friend."

"Aunt Ellen isn't going to like it."

"So who's going to tell her?"

"Grandma!"

Grandma stood up. "He always comes on Saturdays and Thursdays. And sometimes on Wednesdays. I want you to meet him this Saturday. You can walk over with me. And now, let's go make that pizza."

Chapter

15

A FEW WEEKS after Ron began tutoring her in algebra, Mr. Harper gave another test. This time, Olivia managed to get a 42.

"You see," Ron gloated. "You're definitely making progress. "Look!" He pointed to one of the problems she had solved correctly. "See how you applied the quotient rule here."

Olivia looked. "Where?" she asked.

"Here, in this problem. You knew what you were doing."

"I did?"

Ron began explaining how she had correctly applied

the quotient rule, and suddenly his face was very close to hers. She could feel the heat rising up into the roots of her hair, and she raised her face and waited. Would it happen now? Now! Now! she willed and half closed her eyes.

"But here," Ron said, "in almost an identical problem, you got it wrong. Why was that?"

Olivia opened her eyes and hoped her cheeks weren't suspiciously flushed. "I don't know," she admitted. "I just don't seem to understand . . . anything."

"You do. You do," Ron insisted, patting her hand. "One day it will all come together. You'll see."

Ron's house was nearly on the way to the library. It was just a few blocks out of the way, and Olivia began going in that direction. Ron's house was a corner house with a low fence around the back yard. Most of the time, as she passed, carrying library books whether she ended up at the library or not, she could hear Lulu barking. Once Ron's mother backed her car out of the garage, and another time Olivia saw a UPS man ringing the doorbell. She never saw Ron.

One afternoon, she leaned her elbows on the fence, and looked into the yard. Only Lulu was there, and for a moment or two, each of them just looked at the other.

Then, Lulu came flying over to the fence, barking, her tail wagging furiously. Olivia fled.

But another day, she stayed where she was. After all, a fence did divide them, and even though Lulu kept leaping up as if she wanted to get over, Olivia realized she could not. Lulu's tail kept wagging, and this time, instead of barking, she was whining in a friendly way. She likes me, Olivia thought, surprised. I don't know why, but she does.

"Nice dog," she said finally.

Mom and Nate were going to be married the second Sunday in November.

"It's not going to be a very large wedding," Mom told her. "Just the two of us, our kids, his brother, and a few friends. I'd like you to stand up with me, darling, and be sort of a maid of honor."

"I can't," Olivia said. "Don't ask me because I can't."

"Well, of course I won't insist, but Nate's girls are going to be up there with him during the ceremony, and I thought—"

"I can't, Mom. You know how I feel."

"But how will you feel when you see his kids up there with him?"

"Just don't compare me with them, Mom. Please! You know what I think of them."

Mom said carefully, "They're nice kids, Olivia, and they enjoy spending time with us. Of course, Nate is so much fun. He's coaching them in soccer, and he roller-skates with them."

"I'm not interested in soccer, and if I did ever go roller skating, I certainly wouldn't want to go with my own father."

"I never said one word about your father, did I?" Mom said.

"Not directly, but you meant him."

Mom took a few deep breaths. "Okay! Okay! Let's move on. You don't have to stand up with me during the ceremony, but I'd like to go shopping with you and get you a nice dress."

"The one I wore for Grandpa's funeral still fits."

"Olivia—that's a very nasty thing to say."

Olivia didn't think it was nasty enough. If she couldn't stop the wedding, she just wished she could find something to say that was so nasty Mom would feel some of the misery she was feeling.

The marriage was held in the garden of a restaurant in Mill Valley. If it had rained, the party would have moved inside to one of the private rooms. Olivia prayed hard for rain, but the day turned out clear and warm. Nate's brother drove her and Nate's kids to the wedding, and she had to listen to the three of them talking and laughing about people she didn't know. Finally, Nate's older daughter, Alison, who was twelve, said to her, "I think your mother is great."

There was an awkward pause in which she knew she was supposed to say something like "And I think your father's great too." But she didn't, and she wouldn't.

"She's beautiful, too," said Beth, who was nine.

Another awkward pause, and then Nate's brother, whose name was Mike, asked, "So, Olivia, are you interested in becoming a lawyer, too, like your mother?"

"No," she said firmly, "I'm not at all interested in becoming a lawyer."

"I'll bet you're artistic, like your father," Mike said.

Olivia took a second look at him. She was sitting diagonally behind him in the car. Alison was sitting next to him in the front, while Beth was in the back with her. Mike looked a lot like Nate. Olivia could see that. He was grinning in a way that she felt insulted both her and her father.

"No, I'm not at all artistic, but my father is very talented," she said stiffly.

"Oh, I'm sure he is," Mike said heartily.

"Are we nearly there?" Olivia asked.

At the restaurant, Olivia made sure to sit as far as she could from Mike and the two girls. She found a chair, partly behind a large bush, so she was able to hide her anguished face during the ceremony and close her eyes completely at the end to avoid watching her mother's face, pink with happiness, looking with tender eyes at her new husband.

When it was over, and the guests hurried forward to greet the newlyweds, Olivia remained on her chair behind the bush until Alison came to find her.

"Your mother is looking for you," Alison said.

So she stood up and went along with Alison. Mom grabbed her and kissed her. Her mother's face was unbearably happy. She was wearing a cream-colored suit with a purple blouse. Pinned to her jacket was a wonderful star pin with a large amethyst in the center and diamond rays shooting out of it. Olivia tried not to look at it, because she realized it was a gift from Nate. She could hear a couple she didn't know admiring it. Friends of Nate's, she supposed. But then she realized they could be friends of her mother's. There was a time when she knew all of her mother's friends.

She looked back at her mother, and there was Beth, nestling under Mom's arm, cuddling into her side, as she, Olivia, had once done. And Mom was stroking her arm absentmindedly as she smiled and listened to something one of the wedding guests was telling her.

Olivia felt all alone. She knew that, even though she was standing there in the pretty garden, among the well-dressed wedding guests, she was not a part of the scene. Her mother had married Nate and had moved into a world that no longer included her.

Chapter
16

RON'S MOTHER was standing in front of the house, showing swatches of color to a man on a ladder. She smiled as Olivia moved up the stairs.

"Hello, Olivia. Ron just called. He's on his way back from tennis, and he said you should start on the homework. He'll be back in ten minutes. Go on in, dear. I'm just talking to the painter."

Olivia hesitated.

"What is it, dear? The door is open." She motioned to the open door.

"Lulu?" Olivia asked hesitantly. "Is she . . . ?"

"Lulu? Oh, that's right. She's in the backyard. She won't bother you."

Olivia walked up the stairs, dropped her book on the dining-room table, and looked around the room. This was the first time she had ever been alone in Ron's house, and she felt almost embarrassed. She touched the back of the chair that Ron generally sat on and felt how lucky she was to have him in her life. Then she noticed a bunch of pictures hanging up on one wall and moved closer to inspect them. One was of Ron in action on the tennis court, leaping in the air, his arm upraised, ready to slam the ball back across the net. How good looking he was, how muscular, how graceful, and how kind and considerate! Olivia daydreamed contentedly for a few seconds —seeing herself on a tennis court, whipping the ball back over the net to an astonished, admiring Ron, who finally leaps over the net to take her into his arms. Which was really highly unlikely, since she didn't play tennis.

She wandered into the kitchen and looked out the door window overlooking the yard. Lulu lay sleeping in a small sunny spot at one end. The rest of the yard was in shade. There was a broken basketball hoop on one side of the yard, a crooked picnic table, and a few rusted chairs. It didn't look as if the family used the yard very much. Olivia wondered if Lulu followed the sun around all day long—and if she felt cold when the sun finally disappeared from the yard altogether.

Olivia stood very close to the door window, and suddenly Lulu leaped up and came flying up the stairs, barking deliriously.

Olivia quickly backed away, terrified, but even though she could no longer see Lulu, she could hear how her barks turned into a pathetic whine.

"She's lonely," Olivia thought. "She wants me to let her in." Without thinking, she drew close to the door and looked out again.

Lulu jumped up and down outside.

"No, no, Lulu," Olivia said. "No, I can't let you in, but . . ."

Lulu's tail was wagging furiously. There was a desperate, pleading sound in her barking now.

She really likes me, Olivia thought. And she's so little. She just wants some attention. Poor thing! How is it possible, she wondered, that Ron, kind and considerate Ron, should be so thoughtless about Lulu?

Olivia's hand was actually on the doorknob when she heard Ron call out, "Olivia! I'm home."

She hurried back into the dining room, and there he was, out of breath and dazzling in his white tennis clothes.

"I'm really sorry, Olivia," he said, trying to catch his breath. "but I'll make up the fifteen minutes—not today, because Julia's coming at five, but at your next lesson."

"It's all right," Olivia told him. "You run over sometimes when you don't have another student, so just forget about it.

"You're a good sport." Ron smiled, showing his white teeth.

There has to be some part of him that isn't perfect, Olivia thought.

"Why don't you get started on the homework? I'll be right with you."

Listlessly, Olivia began working on her homework assignment. As usual, it was hard to focus on what she was doing, and Lulu's barking was distracting. Ron tried to explain monomials and polynomials and how to solve problems by using the FOIL method, but nothing made any sense at all.

"I don't think I'm ever going to understand algebra," she told Dad that evening.

Dad's computers were flickering and flashing lights all over the walls of his room. Even his face had patches of changing colors.

"I wish I could help you, honey, but I'm really tied

up these days. Maybe your teacher could find a tutor for you," he said, looking at her, but still, absentmindedly, pressing buttons on the nearest computer. A riot of maps opened and closed on the screen.

"Wait! Wait! I'll just straighten it out."

"Oh, Dad! I have a tutor, and he's really great. He says that most of his students, sooner or later, make some kind of progress, even if they never totally master algebra. That's what he said. And he also thought that maybe if I came three times a week, I might really improve. Dad, are you listening?"

"Oh, sure, honey." He jerked his eyes away from the screen, and nodded at her. "You know I used to be pretty good at algebra. And come to think of it, I do have an algebra program that might help you."

Olivia thought about Ron and his house and never going back again, and she panicked.

"Oh, no, Dad, I think I'd better stay with Ron. Mr. Harper is only going to give two more tests in December and one more in January, so it won't be for much longer. It's only for the rest of the term, and if you don't want to pay for the lessons, Dad, I'll pay. Dad! Dad! Are you listening?"

Chapter 17

IN DECEMBER, Grandma decided to invite John Cheney for Shabbat dinner. Nowadays, Grandma had resumed all the cooking and most of the shopping and housework. Mrs. Frobish came only on Wednesdays to help out, as she had before Grandpa died.

"Who is John Cheney?" Aunt Ellen asked Olivia over the phone a few days before Shabbat. "Your father says he doesn't know. Lately your father doesn't seem to know about anything."

"He's busy all the time with his computers," Olivia said. "It's hard to talk to him."

Aunt Ellen sighed. "Now that we don't have to worry about your grandmother, I think we'll have to focus on your father. Maybe he needs to go for a physical. I'll have Uncle Dan talk to him. Anyway, do you know who John Cheney is?"

"He's a friend of Grandma's," Olivia said carefully.

"He is? That's funny—I don't remember hearing his name. Hmm! Cheney? Cheney? There was a man whose last name was Chanin—an associate of Grandpa's—but I'm sure his name wasn't John."

"No. This is somebody Grandma met down at Spreckels Lake."

"Oh!" said Aunt Ellen. "One of those Russian Jewish immigrants, I guess. John Cheney? That's a funny name for a Russian, isn't it?"

"Grandma's cooking a brisket, and she's making her apple cake."

"Mm! I'm so glad she's cooking again, Olivia. And while I have you, tell me how your mother is. I never really talked to you about the wedding. But if you'd rather not . . ."

"I hated it. I don't like Nate, and I don't like his kids—but there's nothing I can do about it. I guess she's fine."

"What was she wearing?"

"Some kind of cream-colored suit and a purple blouse with a big, splashy pin he gave her. It was ugly."

"She looked so beautiful when she married your father. Then she just wore an inexpensive little Mexican dress and a wreath of fresh flowers in her hair. Of course her mother carried on—she never thought much of your father, and the way she cried at the wedding, you'd have thought it was a funeral."

"Please Aunt Ellen, I don't want to talk about her wedding—either one."

"Sure, Olivia, I know how you feel. Well, how's everything else?"

"I think I'm failing algebra."

"But that's incredible," said her aunt. "You're so good in all your other subjects. Maybe you just need some tutoring."

"I have a great tutor," Olivia told her, "but I'm not sure even he can help me. But do grades matter?"

"A great deal," said Aunt Ellen. "You'll be applying to different colleges in a couple of years, and you just have to keep your average up. I keep telling Judy that. But maybe you can work on your algebra during the Christmas break."

"That's what I'd like to do," Olivia said. "Maybe my tutor could give me a lesson every day."

"That's a good idea."

Olivia hesitated.

"Was there something else, dear?"

"Well, I was just wondering."

"Uh-huh?"

"Well, when you met Uncle Dan, did he like you right away?"

"No, I don't think he did. I certainly didn't like him, I can tell you that."

"Well, how did you get him to like you?"

"Oh, Olivia, it was centuries ago. I hardly remember. Anyway, it's five thirty, and I have to go pick up Seth from soccer practice. Give my love to Grandma, and just work a little harder on the algebra."

"I think I really need to concentrate on algebra over Christmas," Olivia told Ron.

"That's a great idea," he said. "I'm sure if you go over all the lessons in the book, starting from the beginning, something will click. It certainly won't hurt trying."

"Well, I wondered if you'd be able to give me some extra lessons?"

"I'd be glad to, Olivia, except I won't be around during Christmas. My family always takes a couple of weeks vacation up at Tahoe. We rent a cabin, and all of us go skiing."

Olivia tried not to look desperate. "All of you are going?" she asked.

"Oh, sure. Jeff loves skiing too, and sometimes we bring friends," Ron said, looking away and smiling.

Stay cool, Olivia told herself, also smiling. Try to act natural, and if he asks you, just take your time before saying yes.

"Yes. I'm asking Julia Ross. She's the girl who comes for a lesson after you. She and I— Well, she's a good skiier, and so she'll be coming up with me."

"Oh!" Olivia could feel her smile wobble, and it was all she could do to keep it straight.

"So I won't be able to give you any lessons until I come back."

"Uh-huh." Olivia was thinking desperately. Just keep the conversation going, she told herself. Don't let him see how you're really feeling. "And . . . uh . . . when will you be leaving?"

"The day school ends. My father wants to take off later that afternoon."

"So," Olivia continued, "all of you—your whole family will be going?"

"Uh-huh. All of us—and a couple of friends."

"And . . . and . . . Lulu?" Olivia was running out of ideas.

"Lulu? Oh, her! I guess she'll go to a kennel, like she always does when we're away. Nobody wants her along. Nobody can stand her."

John Cheney wore a suit with a shirt and tie. His hair was pressed close to his head, and he looked uncomfortable. Grandma, on the other hand, bubbled.

"Have another slice of meat, John."

"No, thank you."

"How about some more potatoes? A little more cauliflower?"

"No, really—it's delicious, Lily, really delicious. But I can't eat anymore." He looked helplessly around the table at all the faces watching him.

"She always tries to make people eat more than they want," Olivia explained. "You'd better just say yes, and then you can make believe you're eating it—very slowly. As long as you have something on your plate, she won't bother you too much."

Grandma laughed. "You see, John, how they pick on me in my own family. I warned you, didn't I?"

"So, John," said Uncle Dan, "you make model boats, Lily says. Do you do it from kits or start from scratch?"

"Oh, he starts from scratch. He wouldn't even look at a kit," Grandma said. "And you should see some of the younger men, the beginners and even a few more experienced ones. They crowd around him like he's a real guru."

"Now, Lily," John said, shaking his head. "We all trade tips. I'm nothing special."

"And—and—you met my mother-in-law down at Spreckels Lake?"

"Yes," John said, smiling over at Olivia, and looking suddenly more comfortable. "It's quite a story, but you should ask Olivia. I never thought she'd forgive me."

Later, Olivia thought Aunt Ellen would never forgive either her or Grandma.

"I don't know why you couldn't have told me who he really was," Aunt Ellen said to Olivia.

Grandma was downstairs, saying good-bye to John.

"You really didn't ask me," Olivia said.

"Now, Olivia, you just let me run on and on, thinking he was one of the Russian immigrants. You could have told me the truth. I don't know why you had to be so evasive. Why wouldn't I be pleased to think my mother had made a nice friend?"

Grandma returned to the dining room, looking particularly cheerful. "Well?" she asked them all, still assembled around the table. "What do you think of him?"

"Oh, he seems very pleasant," Uncle Dan said quickly. "A very pleasant man."

"I never saw him dressed up before," Olivia said. "He looks different. I think he looks better in his casual clothes."

"He thought you all were very nice," Grandma said. "He told me Adam promised to get him a computer listing of all the dealers who stock the woods he's been having trouble finding. Of course, he thinks Olivia is great, but he enjoyed meeting Judy, Seth, and Zack, too. Wasn't it nice how he offered to show them how to operate his boats?"

"Mama," Aunt Ellen asked, "what is going on?"

"I don't understand what you mean?" Grandma put her hands on her hips and leaned in Aunt Ellen's direction.

"I think you do," said Aunt Ellen. "What was all the mystery about here? How come none of us except Olivia knew you were involved with this man?"

"I'm not involved with any man," Grandma said. "And I don't like your tone, Ellen."

"Why wouldn't we all be happy to know you made some new friends, Mama? Haven't I been after you for months and months to get out more and meet some new people—some new, suitable people?"

"Get to the point, Ellen. I'm waiting."

"All of a sudden, this strange man comes for dinner, Mama, and you never said one word to any of us. And neither did Olivia."

"Since when can't I invite a friend to my own house for dinner?" Grandma's eyes narrowed.

"Mama," Aunt Ellen said, coming finally to the point, "I want you to have friends, but just let me remind you what you always told me and everybody else in this family."

"And what was that?"

"Well, to be perfectly blunt, you always told me that I must never even think of marrying a man who isn't Jewish."

"Is that all?" said Grandma, taking her hands off her hips and smiling again. "Well, you don't have anything to worry about then, because I'm not planning to marry him."

Chapter

18

MOM REFUSED to take no for an answer. "You are coming with us to Cabo San Lucas during the break. There's no reason for you not to come, and I know you'll have a wonderful time."

"But, Mom, I can't," Olivia insisted.

"Why not?"

"Well, I have a lot of plans during the holidays."

"Like what?"

"Well, I have to study my algebra."

"You can study down there."

"And Grandma . . ."

"Yes, what about your grandmother? It sounds as if she has plenty of her own plans."

"Well, but she likes me to come along with her. And John, that's her friend, he's making a new little coal barge, and maybe I'll help him paint it."

"That really sounds like a lot of fun," Mom said. "Hanging out with a bunch of senior citizens and painting model boats."

"And Dad. He and I . . ."

"Yes? What kind of plans do you and Dad have for the holidays? Hiking in Point Reyes? Partying at the Fairmount? Going to a bunch of shows? What's he up to anyway lately?"

Olivia tried to make it sound exciting. "Well, he's working on a new, special, educational software program—I think with maps—and there's a school district in Iowa that's really interested."

"Olivia," Mom said, "you are coming with us to Cabo San Lucas, and that's that!"

Grandma and Dad weren't any help at all. Grandma and John were all wrapped up in plans for a big open house at the lake clubhouse, and Dad actually said he thought it was a good idea for her to go.

A couple of days after Christmas vacation started,

Olivia walked past Ron Kramer's house on the way to the library. This time, she really was going to the library. She needed to take out a bunch of books to bring with her so that she'd have something to hide behind during her week in Cabo San Lucas. In a few days, she, Mom, Nate, and his kids were scheduled to fly down.

She paused in front of the house. Nobody else was in sight on the street except for a police car parked half a block away. For a change, she could stand there as long as she wanted, and she began daydreaming about going to Lake Tahoe with Ron and his family. There she came, flying down a steep, snowy slope, wearing a brilliant pink-and-purple outfit, zigzagging around one tree after another, while Ron Kramer, laughing, his white teeth flashing in his tanned face, skiied right behind her. Of course, Olivia did not ski and had never really wanted to ski.

Somebody barked.

All of them were skiing in her daydream—Mr. and Mrs. Kramer, Jeff Kramer, too—but none of them as gracefully as she and Ron, way out in front, cheeks glowing as the fresh winds blew in their faces.

Another bark.

Olivia came down out of her daydream and listened.

That was strange. It sounded as if it were Lulu barking, but, of course, Lulu had been consigned to a kennel two days ago. It must be some other dog.

A few more barks came, unmistakably, from the Kramers' backyard.

It couldn't be—she must be hearing things—and yet, there it was again—a dog barking and barking and, yes, it sounded just like Lulu.

Olivia leaned on the fence and looked down. Lulu looked up at her. A moment passed and then Lulu's tail began wagging. She ran over to the fence and tried to jump up onto it, barking furiously. "Lulu?" Olivia said. "What are you doing here?" Then Lulu began whining— a sad, forlorn whining that Olivia found unbearable.

She leaned her elbows on the top of the fence and tried to figure out what had happened. By this time, Lulu was hysterically leaping up and howling. Olivia surveyed the messy yard and spotted two empty dog dishes. Then she understood what had happened.

"They forgot about you," she whispered to Lulu. "They just went off and left you all by yourself without food and without water."

Lulu was alternately whining and howling.

"But that's terrible!" Olivia wailed. "Oh, that's terrible! You'll be dead before they come back. How could they do it to you?" She began crying helplessly, and Lulu joined her, howling even louder than before.

"What seems to be the trouble, young lady?" a voice called out.

Olivia turned, still propped up on the fence, tears rolling down her face, and saw a policeman looking up at her from the police car which had moved in front of the Kramer's house.

"Oh, officer," Olivia cried, "I'm so glad you're here. You've got to help me." She ran toward the car. There was another, younger, policeman sitting next to the driver who said, "What's wrong?"

"It's Lulu," Olivia wept. "That poor dog in the yard. She belongs to somebody I know from school. But he and his family went away on a vacation two days ago. She was supposed to go to a kennel, but they forgot all about her, and she's still here."

"Well, why don't you call the SPCA," said the driver. "They'll send somebody out."

He started up the car, but before he could pull away, Olivia cried out, "Oh, please! You have to help me! Oh, please!"

"They will help you." The policeman smiled encouragingly. "They'll keep her at the animal shelter until your friends get back."

"Oh, but, officer, she's been without food or water for two days. Two whole days. And she's only a little dog. Suppose they don't come until tomorrow. She could be . . . could be dead." Olivia burst into loud sobs.

"Okay! Okay!" said the officer. "Just calm down. It's going to be all right."

"Let's see what we can do," said his companion. "It really bugs me how people abuse animals."

They parked the car, and both of them ended up peering over the fence with Olivia. When Lulu saw the two policemen, she went scurrying under the staircase, squealing in terror.

"She's afraid of you," Olivia explained, "but she knows me, and she likes me."

"It really is a shame," said the younger policeman, "that people can treat a poor, helpless animal this way. Just look at those empty dishes."

"Well, let's make sure," said the older officer. He strode up the stairs of the house and rang the bell. Nobody answered.

"Let's try their neighbor," said the younger one, ringing the bell of the house next door. Nobody answered, but Olivia noticed that somebody pulled up a shade in one of the upstairs rooms.

"Somebody's home," she informed the police. "I just saw a shade pulled up."

"Please open the door," shouted the younger officer. "It's the police."

It took a few minutes, but the door was finally opened by a very angry, middle-aged woman.

"I was napping," she said, "and you woke me up."

"I'm very sorry, ma'am, but we want to check on your next-door neighbors. Could you tell us if they left on a vacation a couple of days ago and if that's their dog in the backyard?"

"That's their dog all right," said the woman, coming out the door. "And to tell you the truth, that dog woke me up from my nap. That dog always wakes me up. Sometimes they leave it out all night, and it starts barking at five in the morning."

"Well, do you know if they've gone away for a couple of weeks? Did they tell you they were going?"

"They didn't tell me anything, because I don't talk to them. They're the worst neighbors anybody could have. If their stupid dog isn't barking, their stupid kids are making a racket."

"Well, thank you very much, ma'am. I won't bother you anymore."

"And it's not like I haven't called the police lots of times about that dog, and the kids, too—and this is the first time you've ever bothered to come out."

"We'll take care of it, ma'am," said the younger officer, backing down the stairs.

"Just make sure you do!" she said, slamming the door.

Lulu had continued barking during the whole exchange, and Olivia, propped on the fence, began offering words of comfort. "It's all right, Lulu—we'll rescue you. Don't be frightened. We're here to help you. Good dog! Poor dog!"

"Well, I don't know," she heard the older policeman say. But then, Olivia did know. "I'll take her home with me," she offered. "I'll keep her until they come home."

"Mmm!" he said. "I think we'd better call the SPCA. Too bad it's so late in the afternoon, but maybe they'll come anyway."

"But, officer, she knows me!" Olivia pleaded. "And I'll take good care of her. Please!"

"No harm in that," said the younger man. "We'll leave them a note with the girl's name and number. And we'll also give them a citation for disturbing the peace. And maybe we'll give them another one for cruelty to animals."

Later, it seemed so incredible and yet so natural. The

young cop helped her over the fence, and Lulu leaped—actually leaped—into her arms and began licking her face. And she laughed and hugged Lulu, and she wasn't afraid at all.

She rode home in the police car, and all the way Lulu licked her face and yipped happily while she patted Lulu's curly head and hugged her tight. Olivia felt so happy, she didn't realize until later that, finally, she had found a perfect reason not to go on the trip to Cabo San Lucas.

Chapter
19

OLIVIA CALLED Laura as soon as she arrived home.

"Laura," she shouted into the phone, "I have a dog."

"Oh, sure," Laura said, "and it's April Fool's Day."

"No, really, Laura—I have a dog. It's Lulu. You know I told you Ron and his family were going to Tahoe? He said they were going to put Lulu in a kennel, but they forgot. They actually forgot all about her and left her in the yard. For two days she's been there without any food or water. But then these nice cops came along—"

"Wait a minute," Laura said. "Is this all for real? You actually stole a living dog out of the Kramer's yard?"

"I didn't steal her," Olivia insisted, watching Lulu sniff

her way around Grandma's feet. "The cops helped me, and they brought me home in a police car, and I held her—"

"You held a dog! I don't believe it!"

"Honestly! And she kept licking my face. And she's very happy here with me, and not at all homesick. Why should she be—the way they treated her?"

"And what about your father and your grandmother?"

"Oh, my father doesn't care. He says he'll go out and pick up some dog food once you tell me what to get. And Grandma—Grandma likes dogs. She always wanted one, but Grandpa was allergic. Listen! Listen! Grandma's laughing because Lulu just jumped up on the sofa."

"You'll have to train her not to do that," Laura said. "You have to teach her she's not top dog, or she'll be spoiled rotten. What you have to do is hold her down, get her on her back, hold her head, and make her look straight into your eyes. Then she'll know you're the boss. Todd and I had to do that with Henry. He used to push us out of our beds and crowd us off the sofa."

"Oh, I couldn't do that," Olivia said. "She's been through a terrible experience. She's still afraid I'm going to abandon her. Like just before—she had to go, so I opened the door to our yard, and she stayed near the door whining. She was afraid I was going to leave her out there the way those Kramers did. I had to go out with her and stay with her all the time she was outside."

"She'll have to get used to it, won't she? Especially since you'll be going to Cabo San Lucas in a few days."

"Oh—that's right. Well, I just can't go now," Olivia said.

"I don't think your mother's going to appreciate hearing that. I'm sure your grandmother or your father could look after her while you're gone."

Lulu jumped down from the sofa, and resumed her inspection of the room.

"No! I'm not going to leave her. I can't!"

"Well, you'll have to work it out with your mom. But if you are going to be in town, you can come to my concert. That will only be for a few hours, and I'm sure Lulu can manage. And besides . . ." Laura hesitated.

"Besides what?"

"Alan is going to be performing, too. So maybe afterwards, you, Alan, and I can go have a pizza or something."

"Oh!"

"Or we can bring it back to your house if you're going to worry about Lulu. Anyway, Alan is also going to be transferring to Music and Art in February."

"You mean you've definitely decided to transfer?" Olivia said slowly. "You never said it was definite. I . . . I'm going to miss you."

"I'll miss you, too, Olivia, and I don't want you to start thinking this is going to be the end of our friendship."

Olivia didn't say anything. No, she thought, it won't be the end, but Laura will no longer be there for her every day, just as Mom was no longer there.

Lulu rubbed herself against Olivia's leg. Olivia bent down and picked her up. Lulu licked her hand and then settled herself comfortably in Olivia's lap.

"Olivia?"

"I'm still here, Laura. Look, I can't pretend I'm happy you're going." She began stroking Lulu's head.

"We'll see each other. You know that."

"Maybe," Olivia answered. "At least we can meet at the dog run in the park."

"Oh, Olivia, we'll be getting together more than that. Besides," Laura said, "Lulu is not your dog. When the Kramers return, you'll have to give her back."

"I won't," Olivia said. "They're mean to her. They left her to die without food or water. She doesn't miss them at all." Lulu was now curled up, sleeping comfortably, on her lap. "Anyway, I need you to tell me what kind of dog food to get her. We gave her two bowlfuls of water, but the poor thing hardly drank anything. She was so happy to be here with us. Even my father came out of his room to play with her. And he says he'll go right out and buy whatever kind of dog food you recommend."

After Olivia hung up and gave Dad his instructions, she took a deep breath and called Mom at her office. As usual, Mom hardly ever left before seven.

"Hi, darling," Mom said. "Are you getting ready for the trip?"

"Well, I was, Mom, but something came up."

"Are you all right?"

"I am, but, Mom, I won't be able to go."

"Why not?" Mom's voice was not pleasant.

"Because I have a dog, and, Mom, I can't leave her." Olivia began speaking very quickly. "She's an abused dog. She was left alone in a yard without food or water by these awful people who just took off on a vacation and forgot all about her. Mom, two nice cops helped me rescue her, and now I have her here, and I just can't leave her. She's been through a lot. These terrible people never took care of her properly, and—"

"Olivia," said her mother, very distinctly, "we have already paid for your air tickets to Mexico, and if you don't go, we will not get our money back."

"Maybe somebody else can go," Olivia said. "I'm sorry Mom. I'm not going to be able to leave Lulu."

Mom said a few more things before she hung up. But Olivia had no time to think about their conversation, because the phone rang. This time, it was Ron.

"Olivia," he said, "will you please tell me what is going on?"

"Did the police call you up at Tahoe?" Olivia asked, confused. "Or did that neighbor of yours? No—I guess not, because she said she isn't talking to your family."

"She is now," Ron said grimly. "And we're not in Tahoe, Olivia. We're in San Francisco, and we weren't planning to leave until tomorrow."

"But you told me you were leaving the same day school ended," Olivia squealed. "You said your father wanted to start out that same afternoon."

"We changed our plans," Ron said in the same grim voice, "and none of us was home until half an hour ago."

"Oh, no!"

"And there we found two citations from the police department, and our neighbor, crazy Mrs. Fell, was only too happy to explain, in a very loud voice before a number of other interested neighbors, how the police finally agreed with her that we all were a bunch of criminals and a disgrace to the whole neighborhood. Olivia, will you please explain to me what happened."

"Oh, Ron! Olivia groaned. "I thought your family had left for Tahoe, and I was on my way to the library—"

"But you don't pass my house on the way to the library from your house. It's three blocks in the other direction."

"I had another errand," Olivia mumbled. "So I heard Lulu barking, and I thought—I thought maybe you had forgotten her. So two policemen happened to turn up, and I offered to take her. So they helped me climb over the fence, and—"

"But I thought you hated dogs. I thought you were terrified of dogs."

"Not anymore. But, anyway, I thought you had forgotten to take her to the kennel, and I thought since there wasn't any food or water in her dishes, she would die, and . . . Oh, Ron, I don't know what to say."

"You ought to hear what my mother has to say, Olivia. She's not only angry at you but also at the cops. She's thinking of suing you and them."

"Oh, Ron, I'm so sorry. What can I do?"

"Do? Well, you're certainly going to have to apologize to her."

"Oh, yes, I will, I will," Olivia agreed.

"And then you'll have to straighten all this out with the cops."

"Yes, I will."

"You might be the one who ends up with a few citations yourself. And for right now, you'd better bring Lulu back."

"No!" Olivia said.

"What was that?"

"No! I won't bring her back."

"I can't believe this," Ron said. "I always knew you were kind of off the wall, Olivia, but I didn't believe you were this nutty."

"Listen, Ron," Olivia shouted into the phone. "I'll do everything else you say. I'll apologize to your mother, to your father, to your brother, and to you, too. I'm sorry, Ron. I'll apologize to your neighbor, and I'll apologize to the two cops. But I want to keep Lulu. I love Lulu. My grandmother and my father, they're willing for me to have her. We'll take good care of her and make her happy. Nobody in your family cares at all for Lulu."

"Is this for real?" Ron was saying.

"You said so yourself. You said you couldn't stand her—that she was a dumb dog. And Jeff doesn't have time to take care of her. You said nobody could stand her. So let me have her. Give her to me. I'll pay you for her. I'll buy her from you. What do you want for her?"

Now Olivia was crying noisily. "Please don't take her away!"

She was making so much noise that Lulu woke up from her nap, jumped off Olivia's lap, and began running around in front of the phone, barking furiously at it.

"Just hang on a minute, Olivia," Ron said. "And . . . and try to come back to Planet Earth. I'll be right back."

Olivia threw her arms around Lulu, who licked her face and yowled. "I won't let you go," she whispered. "I'll run away with you. I'll hide. I'll leave the country."

"What's going on here?" Dad asked. He had just returned from shopping and was carrying a huge bag of dog food.

"Who are you talking to? Who's getting you so upset?" Grandma demanded. "Is that your Aunt Ellen? Let me talk to her."

"Olivia?" Ron said.

"Yes,"

"My mother says, 'Good riddance!' "

"What?"

"Good riddance to Lulu and to you. And my mother says she doesn't need you to apologize to her or to anybody else in my family. And I don't want to tutor you anymore, either. You're a hopeless case—all around. So just keep away from all of us."

"Oh, yes, I will. I will," Olivia promised. "And thank you, Ron, thank you. I just want to tell you that I appreciate—"

"Oh, bug off!" Ron said, and hung up.

"Who *was* that?" Grandma asked.

"Oh, this wonderful boy—Ron Kramer. No, he's not wonderful. He's a louse. But he tried to teach me algebra, and he's letting me keep Lulu. He smiles all the time, and he's got very white teeth, but they're too big, and I can't stand him."

"His grandmother smiles all the time, too," Grandma said thoughtfully, "and I always thought her teeth were too big."

Chapter

20

FOR THE NEXT week, Olivia read a number of books on dogs and dog care. She learned to identify various breeds. Lulu was evidently mixed but mostly miniature poodle. She learned about canine disorders, hot weather hazards, choking, convulsions, exercise, and grooming.

"She smells like moldy cheese," Grandma said after a week had passed. "I think she needs a bath."

Lulu's black fur was not only smelly, it was also grimy and matted. Evidently the Kramers had not bathed her in a very long time.

" 'How To Bathe a Dog,' " Olivia read in one of her books. There were fifteen steps the author listed. Most of them were simple. First, you had to prepare the bathroom by spreading out towels and newspapers on the floor. Then the author recommended wearing old clothes and filling the tub with warm, not hot, water.

But after Olivia had followed all the simple instructions, her courage failed her.

"Grandma, would you help me, please," she asked. "I've never given anybody a bath before."

"There's nothing to it," Grandma said. "Just remember that you're the one in charge."

"The author of the book suggests treating the dog to a dog biscuit after the bath," Olivia told her, "but maybe I should give her one both before and after."

"Absolutely not!" Grandma said. "Just be firm and teach her that she has to have a bath—period. I bet she'll love it."

"You will look very beautiful," Olivia whispered into Lulu's ear as she carried her into the bathroom.

"Close the door," Olivia whispered to Grandma as she attempted to put Lulu gently into the tub. "The author says it's important for the dog to realize that she can't escape."

But Lulu refused to accept her fate. As soon as Olivia put her into the tub, Lulu began yowling and managed to leap up out of the tub into Olivia's arms.

"You have to be firm," Grandma said. "You have to tell her she has no choice. Your Aunt Ellen always used to put up a fight over baths, but I just put my foot down."

"You do it, Grandma." Olivia handed the struggling dog over to her grandmother. "I'm so glad you're here. I really need you."

"Now, you just behave yourself," Grandma scolded, as she tried to put the dog into the tub. "Now you just listen to me, Lulu. I'm not going to put up with— Olivia! Olivia! Don't let her get out! Olivia!"

But even with the two of them holding on to her, Lulu managed to wiggle her way out of the tub, splashing water all over the bathroom, and all over Olivia and Grandma.

"You'll have to take her to a professional groomer," Laura told her over the phone later that evening. "There's a good one on Balboa, and she knows how to handle dogs—even badly trained ones like Lulu. But she's not cheap."

Lulu put up a fight when she was led into the groomer's shop, tugging at her leash and yowling pitifully.

"Why don't you come back in about an hour," said

the groomer, a cruel, evil-looking woman with dyed red hair and a mean smile.

"I don't know." Olivia hesitated. "Maybe I could come back another day when she's more settled."

"She looks terrible," said the groomer, whose name was Gerri, reaching out a cruel hand with long, sharp fingernails and yanking on the leash. "And she smells even worse."

"She's not used to this." Olivia whimpered, watching Lulu struggle as she was pulled off into what looked like a dark, frightening hole in the back.

"Maybe an hour and a half," Gerri called over her shoulder.

"Could I stay with her, please?" Olivia pleaded.

"It would only be worse," Gerri said, closing the door.

Olivia leaned against the wall of the building next door and thought she would die. What were they doing to poor, terrified Lulu? So what if her fur was grimy, smelly, and matted? Looks weren't everything. What was Lulu thinking now? Was she thinking that Olivia had abandoned her the way the Kramers had? Did she think Olivia was never coming back and that she would be forced to stay with Gerri forever?

Olivia detached herself from the wall and began pacing back and forth in front of the groomer's shop. From time to time, she checked her watch, but time seemed to stand still. She called Grandma, and Grandma said sometimes you had to do things for your loved ones that you knew they hated. Like innoculating children and insisting that they eat foods they didn't like. "But it's for their own good," Grandma said, "and Lulu needs a bath. It's not good for her to be dirty." She hesitated. "Do you really think this Gerri is mean?"

"I do," Olivia said. "She's got a nasty smile and long, sharp fingernails, and she gave Lulu's leash a hard yank."

"Maybe you should go back, and sit in the waiting room," Grandma suggested, "just in case. If I wasn't cooking, I'd come and wait with you."

There were two other people in the waiting room— a man and a woman whose dogs were also being groomed by Gerri. The woman was telling the man how her beagle, Richelieu, had a confrontation with a skunk over a month ago and the smell still lingered. The man said his Kerry blue, Keith, needed to have his toenails clipped every few months, or he ended up with ingrown toenails. Each of the pet owners only seemed to want to talk about his or her own dog and didn't really listen to what the other one was saying. They certainly showed no interest in Olivia. She could hear plenty of barking coming from the inner room but nothing that sounded like an animal in great pain.

After a very long wait, Gerri emerged, carrying an ugly brown-and-white dog. "Well, here's Richelieu," she said, "and he's smelling like a rose." She handed the dog over to his owner, who cuddled him and murmured something loving into his ear.

Olivia stood up. "Is Lulu okay?" she asked in a hoarse voice.

"Oh, yes," Gerri said, smiling rather a nice smile. Her face suddenly did not appear at all cruel. "She is such a darling dog, but I must say her coat has been badly neglected. And, you know, poodles do need regular grooming."

"Well, she wasn't my dog until a week ago," Olivia explained.

"I'm sure you'll see she gets better attention. Just a minute—I'll bring her out."

"The people who had her before weren't very good to her. They left her alone most of the time in their backyard and never took her out for a walk," she told the man who was waiting for his Kerry blue.

"Ttt! Ttt! Ttt!" said the man. "It's very dangerous not to exercise a dog properly. My Keith gets constipated unless I take him out at least once a day."

"Well, Lulu's just a little dog—and some writers say little dogs don't need as much exercise as big dogs—but I take her to the dog run every day. She has a lot of energy, and she loves being with other dogs."

"Sometimes, I take Keith out twice a day. He's a little shy with other dogs, so we walk in the park generally— just the two of us."

Gerri returned, carrying a peaceful Lulu in her arms. Lulu's coat was shining and unmatted, and she looked so pretty, Olivia could not resist saying proudly to her companion, "That's my dog. That's my Lulu."

Mom called after she returned from Cabo San Lucas. She didn't seem at all angry at Olivia—which was good and bad.

"Of course I missed you, and I certainly would have enjoyed myself much more if you had been along," Mom said. But then she went on quickly to describe how beautiful their hotel had been and how much fun the girls had. "They just had a marvelous time and loved the swimming and poking around in the markets. Me, too!"

Olivia tried not to feel jealous. After all, she was the one who had decided not to go, and Mom had said she missed her.

"The girls learned how to bargain, and the three of

us bought identical, matching blouses with stunning embroidery on the sleeves." Mom laughed. "Nate was a real deadbeat at shopping. After a while, we left him by the pool, and the three of us took off together most mornings."

"That's nice!" Olivia said, trying to concentrate on Lulu, nose down, following a spider across the floor.

"And the fruit! The fruit was unbelievable, and none of us got sick."

"That's nice!"

"And the weather! We couldn't have had better weather. What was it like here?"

Lulu nuzzled Olivia's foot and tugged at the bottom of her jeans. What was it like? Olivia hadn't noticed. "Nothing special, I guess. I think it rained one day. Yes, it rained because I couldn't take Lulu out."

"Lulu?"

"My dog. She is my dog now, Mom. Ron Kramer let me keep her." Olivia leaned over and patted Lulu's head. Lulu continued tugging at her jeans.

Mom laughed. "I just cannot believe you've actually gotten over your fear of dogs. It's incredible. And you're really not afraid anymore?"

"Oh, no! And she's such a wonderful little dog. She's so friendly. She likes everybody, but she really loves me the best. When I'm around, she only wants to be near me. She likes Grandma, too, and if I'm not in the house, she'll follow Grandma around. Grandma gives her too many snacks. I guess we all do, and Laura says—"

"Anyway, darling, let's get together this weekend. I have a few souvenirs for you, and Nate will be out of town. As a matter of fact, why don't you come and sleep over?"

"Oh, no, I can't!" Olivia said, and watched Lulu dart meaningfully toward the door to the backyard. Laura kept saying she didn't think Lulu was terribly bright, but who cared? And what did Laura know anyway? Her Henry was certainly no genius.

"Why not? It will just be the two of us this time."

"I couldn't leave Lulu that long."

She waited for Mom to say she could bring Lulu along, but Mom just said impatiently, "That's silly, Olivia. She's just a dog. Your father or your grandmother can look after her."

Lulu was whining at the door, so Olivia said, "Look, Mom, I have to take her out now, but how about a picnic on the beach? You could meet Lulu that way."

"It's supposed to rain," Mom said.

Now Lulu was whimpering. "I'll give you a ring later,

Mom," Olivia said, rising. "I can't talk now. Lulu needs me."

She hung up the phone and hurried across the room. When she opened the door to the backyard, Lulu went scampering down the steps. As Olivia watched her, she forgot about feeling jealous of Mom, Alison, and Beth in their identical embroidered blouses from Mexico.

Chapter 21

OLIVIA USED to have trouble waking up in the morning. Usually the alarm clock went on ringing and ringing before she heard it.

But not anymore. Now Lulu slept on her bed all night. Some time around six, she whimpered softly in Olivia's ear, and Olivia jumped right up, hurried downstairs, and opened the door to the backyard. Sometimes Lulu whimpered at five and, once, at four. It made absolutely no difference. Olivia automatically leaped out of bed and hurried downstairs for Lulu.

"It's ridiculous," Laura told her. "If you're really keeping her, you'd better start training her properly. Maybe you'll have to start training yourself first. She shouldn't be sleeping in your bed, and she certainly shouldn't be waking you up at five or six in the morning. You can get your father—or somebody handy—to saw a dog door into the door leading out to the yard, and you just insist that she go out herself whenever she has to. Even though she is such a birdbrain, she can figure that out, and once she's finished, she can simply come back in through the same dog door she went out. And what's that big black-and-blue mark on your forehead?"

Olivia didn't want to admit that, on the way over to the dog run, Lulu, even though she was on a leash, had taken off in hot pursuit of a cat. "Now, just stop that, Lulu," Olivia called out in the wimpy voice she used whenever she tried to restrain Lulu and which Lulu always ignored. The cat ran very fast, Lulu ran very fast, and so did Olivia, who was trying to keep hold of the leash. Up a tree ran the cat, and Lulu headed straight for it, veering out of the way only at the last moment. But not in time for Olivia to veer out of the way as well, and she ended up smacking right into it, headfirst.

"Oh, I must have banged it on something," Olivia answered evasively, reluctant to listen to any more negative criticism about Lulu.

Everything Lulu did was fascinating and every action

of hers understandable to Olivia. She was not going to train her as Laura suggested, or break her spirit. Certainly she needed to go to the vet for her shots, to Gerri for grooming, and certainly she required nourishing dog food (but a little taste of mint chocolate-chip ice cream —a dish both Lulu and Olivia were particularly fond of —should not upset her stomach). Lulu, as a matter of fact, appeared to have an iron stomach, judging from the extra tidbits Grandma kept feeding her.

When she was away from Lulu, Olivia couldn't wait for them to be reunited. When she was home with the rest of the family, Lulu only wanted to sit in Olivia's lap, or at her feet, or by her side, rising only from time to time, to run howling to the window if something meaningful passed or to greet any guest with loud barks.

"You never let us have a dog or a cat," Aunt Ellen complained. "And I remember how heartbroken I was when a boy in my Sunday School class said I could have a kitten from his cat's litter and you said I couldn't."

"It was because of Papa," Grandma said, giving Lulu a piece of noodle kugel. "He was allergic to cats, dogs, birds—but not turtles. Didn't you have a turtle, Ellen?"

"No, I never did," Aunt Ellen said. But she patted Lulu's head and agreed that she was adorable.

"Is she a lot of work?" her cousin Judy wanted to know.

"Not at all," Olivia told her.

"Ah, don't listen to her," Grandma contradicted. "She gets Olivia up every morning at six, sometimes earlier, to let her out to the backyard. And every day Olivia takes her out to the dog run, and she's always brushing her hair with a special dog brush. She's busy all day long with Lulu, and school hasn't even started up again. But I think it's good for her. It gives her a responsibility, and—Now, you stop that, Lulu! You stop that this second!"

Lulu had taken a dislike to Uncle Dan and came running out from beneath the table from time to time to bark at him.

"Can't you put her out while we're eating?" Uncle Dan suggested.

Olivia picked Lulu up and kept her on her lap, hoping Uncle Dan didn't notice how Lulu licked at any crumbs that fell on the table.

"How old is she?" Zack wanted to know.

"Well, I think she's about four, judging from her teeth. You know I'm not speaking to her old owners. Actually, I guess they're not speaking to me, so I'm really not positive, but Gerri—she's the dog groomer—she thinks Lulu is about four. I'll have a birthday party for her next year, December 19th—that's the day I got her —and you're all invited."

Lulu suddenly leaped out of Olivia's lap and began barking again at Uncle Dan.

"Mom," Seth asked, "can we get a dog, too?"

"Certainly not!" said Uncle Dan.

When school started up again in January, the first thing Olivia noticed as she slid into her seat in Spanish was Jim Morgan's neck with the silver chain around it. She had completely forgotten about boys during the holidays, but maybe things hadn't changed all that much after all. She could feel her internal temperature begin to rise.

He turned and grinned his crooked smile at her. "How're you doing, Olive Oyl?"

"Uh—okay!" He really was cute.

"How'd you enjoy your holidays? I had a blast. . . ." and Jim began describing the parties he'd been to, the friends he'd hung out with, the makeup homework he hadn't done.

"I got a dog," she burst in, not waiting for him to finish.

"No kidding!" he said, grinning even more crookedly. "I've got two dogs—two Labs. I love dogs."

"You do?" Olivia grinned back at him and leaned forward in her seat. "I never had one before."

"What kind of a dog is it?"

"Oh, I guess a mutt—but mostly poodle—a little black miniature poodle. She's really gorgeous. People stop to pet her, she's so adorable."

Jim made a face. "I really don't like poodles," he said. "They're stupid and they make a lot of noise and they're silly-looking."

"I don't think so," Olivia said, leaning back. "I don't think they're stupid at all. So what if they make a lot of noise? Dogs are supposed to make a lot of noise. And I think she's beautiful. You haven't even seen her, so how do you know she's silly-looking?"

The bell rang, and Señora Alvarez, up at the front of the room, began speaking.

Jim Morgan turned around, and Olivia looked disdainfully at the back of his neck, which, she noted, had a disgusting clump of pimples right under his left ear. How could she ever have thought he was cute?

Chapter

22

ON THE LAST day of algebra class, Mr. Harper proceeded to recite the final mark for each student in his class.

"If I could give an A+, I would," he said, smiling at Lisa Ng. "You deserve it, and I hope you go on, and take advanced algebra with me next term."

The worst teacher in the whole school, Olivia decided, and the meanest.

"Ron Kramer—an A, of course. I hope you go on and take advanced algebra with me, too. You'll always be welcome in any class of mine."

Olivia tried for one last time to catch Ron's eye and to smile her pleasure at his success. She wanted to make up with him, but he avoided looking at her, and she supposed she might as well give up.

"Rose Lister—A."

No other teacher of Olivia's had ever announced his students' marks out loud before the whole class. Of course, if you were getting an A, you certainly didn't mind.

"Ryan James—A−."

But if you were going to fail, you didn't want your teacher to rub your face in it. Well, she knew she was failing. She'd never managed to get over a 42 in any test, and she also knew she would have to repeat the class.

"Shannon Means—B."

Somebody had told her that Ms. Sheffield was nasty, too, and so was Mr. Yamasaki. Maybe all algebra teachers were nasty. She'd have to figure something out. She certainly would make sure not to take Mr. Harper again.

"Lester Singh—C+."

She knew she was going to fail—the first time she had ever failed in anything, and probably hers would be the last name Mr. Harper recited. Unless it was Maryanne Rogers, who also never seemed to get a passing mark. She looked over at Maryanne, whose shoulders were hunched and whose eyes were focused down on her desk.

Olivia held her head up straight. Nasty man, to humiliate his students! She resolved that if she ever became a teacher she would never, never humiliate her students the way Mr. Harper was doing.

"Bill Stein—D+. Molly Gin—D. It's hard for me to believe, Molly, that you're actually the sister of Karen Gin, a straight-A student."

Recently Olivia had begun to think of becoming a vet. She smiled. She was wondering what Lulu was doing at this very moment. Maybe she was following Grandma around the kitchen, or sleeping on Olivia's bed.

"Maryanne Rogers—F."

Later, she would take Lulu out to the dog run. Laura wouldn't be bringing Henry today, which was too bad, because Lulu liked Henry, but there were a couple of other dogs she liked, too, that generally were there in the afternoon.

"And last and certainly least, Olivia Diamond—F. I hope you're not planning on taking advanced algebra." Mr. Harper was smiling his nasty smile at her, and the kids were tittering again, as usual.

Olivia smiled back at him. "I might," she said, "but I'll be sure not to take it with you."

"Failed algebra!" Grandma said. "You failed algebra?"

"Uh-huh," Olivia said, putting a leash on Lulu.

"But why didn't you say something? Why didn't you tell me?"

"I did, Grandma, but I guess for a while, you weren't able to listen, and lately you've been busy. It's okay. I'll take it over again."

"But—does your father know?"

"I guess so. Anyway, I'd better go now, Grandma."

"Where? Where are you going?"

"Over to the dog run."

"By yourself? Is Laura taking her dog, too?"

"Not today. She's practicing today. I'll see you later, Grandma."

"Wait! Wait! Maybe I'll go with you."

"That would be nice, Grandma, but you don't have to if you're busy."

"But first, Olivia, let's go say a few words to your father."

"He's busy, Grandma. I don't think he'll want to come with us." But Grandma was on her way up the stairs, and Olivia followed along behind.

Dad was surrounded by his usual blinking lights, whirs, and clicks.

"Adam!" Grandma said angrily, "I have to talk to you."

"In a minute," Dad said, gazing intently at one of his computer screens.

"Right now!" his mother ordered. "And just turn all that stuff off!"

"Turn it off!" Dad repeated. "Turn it off!"

"Your daughter has just failed algebra," Grandma announced.

"Failed algebra!" Dad repeated.

"Stop repeating everything I say," Grandma said. "You're going to have to do something. You're her father, and you need to take some responsibility."

"It's okay, Dad," Olivia said. "I'll have another teacher next term, and maybe I can find a better tutor than Ron Kramer."

"I think I have an algebra program that might help you," Dad said, suddenly smiling and nodding at both her and Grandma. "How about that?"

"Absolutely not," said Grandma. "How about you tutoring her yourself? In person. You used to be very good in math. Papa was very proud of you."

Something clicked in Grandma's throat, and Dad said, slowly, "Yes, I was good in math—and I was very good in algebra."

"Come out of this room," Grandma said. "I don't know how anybody can think with all these things clicketing and clacketing."

Dad came outside and stood blinking at them. "I'm sorry," he said.

"You should be," Grandma told him. "This girl is an honor student—at least, she used to be. And you should be ashamed of yourself. Maybe we should both be ashamed."

"I'll tutor you, Olivia," Dad promised. "I'll try."

"I'm going to try, too," Grandma promised on the way to the dog run. "It's not only your father. He's a genius, and he can't help himself, but I guess I haven't been much help to you either. You spend all your time with Lulu. That's fine. She's a darling, but you have to have friends, and you should be going to parties. Would you like to have a party, Olivia? I'll help you cook. I'll bake my special chocolate cake I used to make when Aunt Ellen had parties. We can have a strawberry punch."

"Oh, Grandma," Olivia said. "I don't want a party.

Not yet. I'd only have Laura and a bunch of dogs to invite. But I'm so glad you're you again."

Olivia watched Lulu racing on the beach. Her little black legs revolved faster and faster as she flew in pursuit of a large Rottweiler. How fearless she was! How confident!

"She certainly has a lot of energy," Mom said. The two of them were sitting, or trying to sit, on a mat and eat the picnic lunch Mom had brought along. Every so often Olivia had to leap up, chase Lulu, and bring her back.

"Can't you put her on a leash while we eat our lunch?" Mom asked crabbily. "She certainly needs to be trained."

Lulu inspected Mom's sandwich, which she was unwrapping on a paper plate.

"Now, stop that!" Mom said. "Can't you make her stop, Olivia?"

"Come over here, Lulu. Come to me. Here, I brought you some nice dog biscuits, and here's your water." Olivia poured a thermos of water into Lulu's bowl. "She gets thirsty when she's overheated," she explained fondly as Lulu noisily lapped the water.

"Anyway," Mom said, "I did have something serious to talk over with you."

Lulu began inspecting Olivia's sandwich, and Olivia broke off a piece of it and began feeding it to her.

"That can't be good for her," Mom said. "It's salami and cheese."

"With pickles," Olivia added. "She eats everything. You should see what Grandma gives her. But she doesn't put on any weight. I guess because she's so active. But, Mom, what did you want to talk to me about?"

"Well, it's about the house—our old house. Do you know what your father plans to do about it?"

Finally, Lulu stretched out on the mat, right next to Olivia, and settled herself comfortably for a nap.

"Olivia, she has a paw in your plate."

"That's okay. Anyway, no, I don't know what he plans to do. Why don't you ask him?"

"I will, but I wanted to know what you thought first. Do you think you—and he—would want to go back?"

"No!" Olivia immediately answered.

Mom nodded. "It has too many memories, I suppose."

"Well, no, it's not that—but the yard's too small."

"Too small?"

"For Lulu, I mean. At least at Grandma's house, she's got a real big yard whenever she feels like running around outside. Although most of the time she stays in, and there's lots of room inside for her to roam around, too. Only Dad doesn't want her in his room when he's away. Grandma doesn't mind if Lulu jumps on her bed, although most of the time she prefers sleeping on mine."

"I can't believe this," Mom said. "For heaven's sake, Olivia, Lulu is just a dog."

"Just a dog?" Olivia repeated. "She's not just a dog. She's my dog, Mom."

"I know. I know. But Olivia, you can't live your life around a dog. In a few years, you'll be going away to school, and—"

"And she'll come with me."

Mom put down her sandwich. "Most colleges don't allow animals in dorms."

"I'll find one that does. Or I'll stay home and go to City College or to State."

"You're being absolutely ridiculous," Mom said angrily.

"I don't think so," Olivia said, gently smoothing Lulu's fur. "I'm happy when I'm around her."

Mom didn't respond. She was slowly chewing her sandwich and looking at the ocean. Suddenly Olivia felt a great sadness between them. She reached out and took Mom's hand. "Mom," she said, "Mom . . ."

"It's all so complicated," Mom said, still looking at the ocean.

"No, it isn't, Mom. It's really working out now, the way you always said it would."

"But not the way I thought. You're different. You're changing in a way that doesn't—well—doesn't include me."

"You mean because of Lulu?"

"Not only Lulu. I'm beginning to think maybe I didn't do the right thing. I'm very happy with Nate, but maybe I should have taken you, too, when I left. Or at least arranged to have joint custody with your dad."

"You didn't want me," Olivia said, feeling a sudden rush of the old, nearly forgotten misery.

"Oh, darling, I did, I did. But I thought you'd be better off with your dad. I've told you that lots of times. I never thought he'd . . . he'd turn into a computer nerd and get lost in cyberspace."

"He said he'll tutor me in algebra. He said he'll try. . . ."

"And then your grandmother. She was always the stable one in the family. I never thought she'd flip out the way she did."

"There's nothing wrong with Grandma now," Olivia

said. "She helps me with Lulu, and she wants me to have parties, and she's going to teach me how to make her special chocolate cake."

"I guess I was too busy trying to make a new life with Nate. But, darling, it's not too late. Why don't you come live with me? You can even bring Lulu."

"I can't, Mom," Olivia said carefully. "It's different now. I don't want to now. I think it's better the way it is."

Mom nodded, and reached over to take her hand. "Well, I will be travelling a lot more in the next few months, so if you really are happy with your father, I won't press you. But maybe I can take you with me when I go to New Orleans in April. Would you like that, darling? We could have so much fun—just the two of us."

Lulu suddenly woke up and took off after a Great Dane that stood a distance away, waiting for her. Olivia leaped up and chased after her so she didn't have to answer Mom. That was just one of the many, many advantages of owning a dog. You could always pretend the dog needed you, and you could put off answering awkward questions.

Chapter 23

ANOTHER DAY, Olivia and Laura watched their dogs chase each other around the dog run.

"It's so different at Music and Art," Laura said. "Every kid is into either music, art, or literature, and most of them are talented."

"Well, that's what you wanted, isn't it?" Olivia said. Henry and Lulu were united now in barking at a snobby-looking Doberman who pretended to ignore them.

"Yes, I guess I do, but it's different. Of course, it's fun having Alan around, but, Olivia, I miss you."

"I miss you, too." Olivia said. "When school first

started up again, I really felt out of it. I didn't know who to eat lunch with or who to talk to. It was terrible."

"I was afraid of that," Laura said.

"But then I found this girl in my English class, who has a corgi, and there's a boy named Fred Johnson, in my algebra class—"

"I know Fred," Laura said. "He's a jerk."

"No, he isn't. He has two pit bulls, and he says they're really misunderstood. Anyway, the three of us are having lunch together most days."

"Well," Laura snapped, "it certainly sounds as if you've had no trouble making new friends."

"I guess not." Olivia agreed.

"I'm happy for you," Laura said.

"But none of them will ever be like you. Anyway, look Laura! Just look at how Lulu and Henry are chasing that Doberman. Isn't it funny?"

"So—anyway, Olivia, what's going to happen with your old house?"

"Dad thinks we should sell it. Mom thinks so, too. We'll stay on with Grandma.

"But suppose she marries John Cheney?"

"She won't. He's not Jewish."

"But he could just come and live with her. Then what?"

"It's a big house," Olivia said.

"You know," Laura said. "It's a funny thing how you've changed. You were such a wimp when your mother walked out, sort of stuck in the past, and now you're—well, different."

"I guess I am," Olivia said. "I'm not miserable anymore, I know that. And I also know it's because of Lulu."

Laura raised her eyebrows.

"I know what you're thinking, and in my opinion, Lulu is just as smart as Henry. Anyway, everything changed after I got her."

"Well," Laura said kindly, "it was good that you got over your fear of dogs. Maybe it also gave you a little more self-confidence."

"Not only that, but it made me think of somebody else—Lulu, I mean. Before, all I could think about was me, how miserable I was and how angry I was at my mother for abandoning me. Then, suddenly, I found I wasn't the only one who was miserable and abandoned."

"Of course, the Kramers didn't exactly abandon Lulu."

"And my mother didn't exactly abandon me. Anyway, my life changed because of Lulu. I even got a seventy-three on my last algebra test."

Laura nodded. "Things have changed for me, too. Look at how I used to be petrified before I performed in any recital. I still sweat a lot, and my heart feels like it's jumping out of my chest. But I can handle it, and I guess it will keep getting better all the time."

"Sure it will," Olivia agreed, watching how Lulu was now sniffing around a little gray-and-white puppy.

"My father is already planning for me to study violin at the Juilliard School in New York when I graduate. He keeps talking about the future. He says seven, eight years down the road I should be ready to play professionally. What about you, Olivia? Do you ever think about the future?"

"Not like you," Olivia sighed. "I don't know what's going to happen to me in the future. Sometimes it's even a little scary thinking about it. But, speaking about the future, my grandmother keeps nagging at me to have a party. She's trying to make a normal girl of me."

"Not much hope for that," Laura said.

"Look who's talking," Olivia said, giving her a friendly shove. "Anyway, maybe I will have one in a few weeks. You're invited, and so is Alan. I guess I'll ask Fred and Wendy—she's the girl with the corgi. My grandmother is dying to help, but I told her the best way she can help is to go out."

"I bet she won't."

"She says she'll stay in the kitchen, but I wouldn't

count on it. Anyway, if you can think of anybody else to ask, let me know."

"What about that cute boy in your Spanish class? You used to like him."

"Jim Morgan? That's ancient history. Actually, there's nobody special right now."

"Is this your dog?" somebody demanded.

Olivia looked up at a boy who was holding a squealing puppy. Lulu was racing around and around at his feet.

"Yes, she is. What's wrong?"

"She's scaring my dog. Here, stop it! Get away!" He waved a stick at Lulu, and Olivia leaped to her feet.

"Don't you dare hit her with that stick," she yelled. "She wasn't going to hurt your dumb dog. She was just trying to make friends."

"I wasn't going to hit her," said the boy.

"She's the gentlest dog in the world," Olivia said angrily, bending down and picking up Lulu. She noticed that the boy was about fifteen or sixteen, and not bad looking.

He put the stick behind him and smiled, almost apologetically.

"This is my first dog," he said, "and maybe I'm a little anxious."

"Lulu is my first dog, too," Olivia explained, smiling

too, and feeling a familiar warmth begin to spread inside her.

"I've only had him for a couple of weeks, but he whines all the time. I have a feeling he may not even like me."

"He probably misses his mother," Olivia told him confidently. "But he'll get used to you. If you're kind to him, he'll come around."

Lulu licked her face, and the boy said, "Your dog certainly seems to like you."

Olivia noticed that he dropped the stick, and she reached over and patted the puppy's head. "Cute little dog!" she said.

Maybe she didn't know what the future had in store for her like Laura, but as Grandma said, there were bound to be some pleasant surprises along the way.

J
Sachs, Marilyn
Another day

15.99

J
Sachs, Marilyn
Another day

JUL 18 1997	5736		15.99
AUG 22 1997	5756		
MAY 05 2003	A 4406		
AUG 28 2009	A 2971		